A Place To Belong

The Orphan Train Quartet

A Place To Belong

Joan Lowery Nixon

BANTAM BOOKS
NEW YORK · TORONTO · LONDON · SYDNEY · AUCKLAND

For Elise Howard
in camaraderie

A PLACE TO BELONG

A Bantam Book / February 1989

*The Starfire logo is a registered trademark of Bantam Books, a division of
Bantam Doubleday Dell Publishing Group, Inc. Registered in U.S. Patent and
Trademark Office and elsewhere.*

Library of Congress Cataloging-in-Publication Data

Nixon, Joan Lowery.
A place to belong / Joan Lowery Nixon.
p.   cm. — (The Orphan train quartet)
Summary: In 1856, having traveled with his young sister from New
York to a foster home on a farm in Missouri, ten-year-old Danny
plots to get his foster father to send for and marry his mother.
ISBN 0-553-05803-7
[1. Foster home care—Fiction. 2. Remarriage—Fiction. 3. Farm
life—Fiction. 4. Missouri—Fiction.] I. Title. II. Series:
Nixon, Joan Lowery. Orphan train quartet.
PZ7.N65p1   1989
[Fic]—dc19   88-7671
                                                             CIP
                                                             AC

Published simultaneously in the United States and Canada

*Bantam Books are published by Bantam Books, a division of Bantam Doubleday
Dell Publishing Group, Inc. Its trademark, consisting of the words "Bantam
Books" and the portrayal of a rooster, is Registered in U.S. Patent and Trademark
Office and in other countries. Marca Registrada. Bantam Books, 666 Fifth Avenue,
New York, New York 10103.*

PRINTED IN THE UNITED STATES OF AMERICA

FG   0 9 8 7 6 5 4

A Note From the Author

During the years from 1854 to 1929, the Children's Aid Society, founded by Charles Loring Brace, sent more than 100,000 children on orphan trains from the slums of New York City to new homes in the West. This placing-out program was so successful that other groups, such as the New York Foundling Hospital, followed the example.

The Orphan Train Quartet was inspired by the true stories of these children; but the characters in the series, their adventures, and the dates of their arrival are entirely fictional. We chose St. Joseph, Missouri, between the years 1860 and 1880 as our setting in order to place our characters in one of the most exciting periods of American history. As for the historical figures who enter these stories—they very well could have been at the places described at the proper times to touch the lives of the children who came west on the orphan trains.

Joan Lowery Nixon

CHILDREN
Without Homes.

A number of the CHILDREN brought from
NEW YORK are still without homes.
FRIENDS FROM THE COUNTRY PLEASE

CALL AND SEE THEM.

▸

MERCHANTS, FARMERS
AND FRIENDS GENERALLY

Are requested to give publicity to the above

AND MUCH OBLIGE

H. FRIEDGEN, Agent.

1

JENNIFER COLLINS RACED down the stairs, nearly colliding with her grandmother. "You can't go jogging because it's raining," Jennifer said, "so could you read some of Frances Mary's journal and tell us now—*right now*—about Danny and Peg and why they couldn't write letters to anyone, and about the attempted kidnapping, and—"

Grandma Briley laughed and held up a hand. "Slow down," she said. "You haven't even had breakfast yet."

"I'll eat fast," Jennifer promised.

Her twelve-year-old brother, Jeff, sauntered into the hall just behind Grandma. "It's oatmeal," he mouthed, as he rolled his eyes and grimaced.

"Even if we're having oatmeal," Jennifer solemnly added.

"You might try it with brown sugar, cinnamon, and butter," Grandma said. "Jeff liked it so much that he ate two helpings. Isn't that right, Jeff?"

"Yeah, I guess I did," Jeff mumbled, looking embarrassed.

"Butter on oatmeal? That sounds strange," Jennifer said.

"That's the old-fashioned way to serve oatmeal," Grandma answered. "I think a recipe from long ago will get you ready for a story that took place in 1860. Don't you?"

Jennifer smiled. She already felt a close relationship with Frances Mary Kelly. Frances, Jenny's great-great-great-grandmother, had written the stories about her trip to the West with her brothers and sisters on one of the orphan trains.

When she had first introduced Jennifer and Jeff to Frances and her journal, Grandma had combed Jennifer's long dark hair into the style worn by Frances so that she would look even more like Frances's photograph. Each time Jennifer had studied the photograph or held Frances's faded blue journal, she had felt a peculiar kind of tingle, as if there were a special bond between them.

"Come with me," Grandma said. "I'll be chef in charge of the oatmeal, and you can pour yourself a big glass of orange juice. The kitchen's as good a place as any to tell Danny's and Peg's story."

It took just a few minutes for Grandma, Jeff, and Jennifer to settle around the kitchen table. Jennifer took a tentative bite of the oatmeal and was surprised to find that she liked it. She watched Grandma gently open the cover of the journal and turn to the page that began Danny's story.

"As I've done before, I'll read just a few paragraphs of Frances's own words," Grandma said. "Then I'll tell you the rest of the story. Are you ready?"

"Yes!" Jennifer and Jeff answered together, so Grandma tilted the journal to the light and began to read the faint, spidery writing.

As I stared back at all those people who had come

to look over the children from the orphan train and perhaps choose one, I hoped with all my might that Danny and Mike would find a home together.

Danny, at ten, was tall and strong for his age and had a careful, well worked out answer for everything. He carried his shoulders back and his chin high. "Stubborn," a few people said about him. "Determined," said others. Everyone agreed, however, that eventually he'd do well for himself. But I saw a vulnerable side of Danny most people couldn't see, and I wasn't as sure.

When Danny was only seven, Da had overheard him explaining to Mike an elaborate escape route back to our home, "just in case those big blokes from Seventeenth Street ever decide to come after us." Da had laughed and said to Ma, "You'll never have to worry about Danny. If the fates ever choose to deal the boy a bad hand, they'll find him well prepared to take care of the problem."

And later, when he had grown old enough to work as a shiner, Danny had come home limping a bit, tugged off his right boot, and proudly dumped a handful of pennies on the table. He had rubbed his sore right foot as he announced, "Those bullies on the Avenue aren't going to get my hard-earned coppers!" Ma had smiled and tousled his curly brown hair, calling him, "My careful, cautious child."

Danny had been very close to Da, and he had suffered terribly the loss of a father when Da died. It wasn't long before he'd attached himself to Mike, and no one could even waggle a scolding finger in Mike's direction without Danny jumping to Mike's defense. Mike—only a year older and an inch shorter than Danny—had such a ready sense of mischief that he seemed an unlikely one to take on the job of father.

Would Da be proved right about Danny? I didn't know. When we learned from the people at the Children's Aid Society that we'd probably be separated and placed with different families, I'd seen the shock and terror in Danny's eyes. He'd edged close to Mike, and I'd heard him say, his voice quivering, "We'll stick together, you and me, huh, Mike?"

I would have given anything to be able to promise Danny then and there that his fear of being parted from his brother was groundless. But I couldn't promise. I didn't know what would happen until that day in the church when a kind couple chose Danny and Peg together. It was a boy and a girl they had come looking for, and there was no room for Mike.

When it was time to leave, little Peg, only seven years old, her face wet with tears, took her foster mother's hand trustingly, but Danny—oh, how I ached to see the misery on his face as he said good-bye to Mike.

"You'll have a good home with these people," I'd told Danny with all the confidence I could muster. But a nagging part of my mind kept scolding, "How can you speak so bravely? How can you possibly know that your words are the truth?"

2

DANIEL JAMES KELLY took his sister's hand and held it tightly. "Stop sniveling, Peg," he ordered. "You don't have to be afraid anymore."

Peg looked up at him and tried to speak, but out came a strangled sob. Her cheeks were streaked with tears, and her eyelids were swollen and red.

Danny felt as miserable as Peg looked. He had convinced himself that he understood why Ma had sent her children west on the orphan train, but now his throat hurt and his eyes stung as he thought about the dream that had ended.

It had been his own dream, one that he hadn't dared share with anyone—even with Mike.

Even though Da had died more than two years earlier, Danny still remembered vividly his father's touch and smile. After a long while, although he still missed Da terribly, the dream began. He'd begun to hope with all his heart that someday his mother would marry again and give him another father. There was a huge, empty place in his life that only a father could fill.

But all that was in the past, and now he and Peg were going to live with strangers.

Andrew MacNair, the tall scout who had brought them from New York City to St. Joseph, Missouri, on the orphan train, stepped forward to say good-bye to Danny and Peg and to the foster parents who had offered them a home. He handed Alfrid Swenson the tightly wrapped bundle that contained Danny's and Peg's belongings. "I'll pay you a visit in about six months," he said. "Have a safe trip home."

Alfrid Swenson was tall and bony. His sparse, pale blond hair topped blue, solemn eyes set in a deeply sunburned face. Alfrid spoke pleasantly to Peg and Danny, but Danny wondered if he ever smiled.

Olga Swenson, on the other hand, had the crinkle lines around her mouth and eyes that came from laughing. Her skin was as pale as the white paper flowers which girls sometimes sold on the street corners in New York. She was tiny and clutched her black wool shawl around her shoulders as though even her bones were cold.

Katherine Banks, who lived in St. Joseph and had been on the train with them, rushed up to Danny and Peg for a last hug good-bye. While Olga stopped to chat with Katherine, Alfrid leaned down to speak quietly to Danny and Peg.

"My wife's health is fragile," he said. "I want her to feel well and strong again. I thought long and hard about what would be best for Olga, and I decided that the laughter of children would be the medicine that would help her most."

Danny nodded. He was heartbroken at having to leave his brothers and older sisters and terrified about going away with strangers, yet at the same time he was terribly

6

afraid that no one would want him and Peg. "You'll find us to be cheerful, sir," he said bravely. "Peg is full of good humor, always able to bring a smile to our mother's face." He gave Peg a poke.

But Peg, hanging tightly on to his hand, her head pressed against his shoulder, gave another hiccuping sob. If Alfrid Swenson wanted laughter, Danny didn't see how in the world he could have picked a less likely pair.

Olga stepped forward and, like a bird tucking a chick under her wing, suddenly enfolded Peg in her black wool shawl, until all that could be seen of Peg was the flaming topknot of her curly red hair. "Come," she soothed. "You're tired, and it's time to take you home."

"Our farm isn't far from St. Joseph," Alfrid told them, as he led the way out of the church and down the street. Danny's curiosity overrode his fear as he stared at the passersby—men dressed in buckskin or in heavy cotton work clothes; women in hoopskirts and small, flowered hats or simple, dark print dresses topped with woolen shawls; buggies, horseback riders, and wagons, large and small, that rumbled and rattled over the deep ruts in the street.

They came to a grand, five-story building with a sign in front that proclaimed it The World's Hotel. Olga, her arm still around Peg, stopped in the middle of the sagging wooden sidewalk. "Alfrid," she said, "let's stop in the hotel for a hot cup of tea before we begin our ride home."

"If that's what you wish," Alfrid replied, and looked at his wife with tenderness. Danny remembered his own father sometimes looking at Ma like that, and the ache in his throat grew worse.

Excitement tipped Olga's cheeks with pink and added a lilt to her voice as she said to Danny and Peg, "The lobby of the hotel is a beautiful place with red Brussels carpets. I want you to see it."

Peg's eyes widened as they entered the huge, paneled lobby with its wide, winding staircase. "It's like a castle in the fairy tales Da told us," she whispered, awestruck.

"And you're the princess," Olga said. "With that blue ribbon matching the blue in your eyes, you're the loveliest little girl I've ever seen."

The dimple in Peg's right cheek flickered, and she stood a little taller. "Can I have sugar in my tea, ma'am? Real sugar?" she asked.

"Of course," Olga said. She led the way between the groups of people who milled through the lobby. Danny stared admiringly as two narrow-waisted women with red cheeks and lips passed him. Their bright dresses had wide skirts held out with hoops, and Danny had to jump aside to get out of the way.

"They're actresses," Olga told Danny and Peg in a low voice. "They're with a traveling theater company that's stopping here on the way to St. Louis."

Peg twisted to stare at the women, and Olga gave Peg's hand a little tug.

A man with a deep, resonant voice called to the two women and strode toward them. Each word was distinct and as musical as though it had been rung by a bell. He was not a tall man, but he held himself so that he seemed tall. As he conversed with the women, he postured and posed, obviously aware that many people in the hotel lobby were watching him.

Alfrid scowled. "I don't like that fellow," he muttered to Olga. "Artemas Gund heard him declaiming in the Buffalo Saloon. He's a rabid Southern sympathizer and antiabolitionist."

"What's that?" Danny asked.

"A man who believes in slavery," Alfrid explained, "and who makes his feelings known even when they are not wanted or asked for."

Danny shivered and looked away from the man. Da

had taught them that slavery was terribly wrong. Life was hard enough without having to belong to somebody else. Danny couldn't imagine being forced to work his whole life for someone who could do whatever he wanted with him. "Do people listen to him?" he asked.

"Only those as foolish as he." Olga sniffed. "The fellow is just an actor—no one important."

"What's his name?" Danny asked.

"Booth," Alfrid said. "John Wilkes Booth."

"Enough of those people," Olga interrupted. "Let's have our tea, and some shortbread cookies with it."

"Cookies?" Peg's expression flashed from delight to concern. "Danny loves cookies, but I do, too," she said. "Don't let him eat them all."

Olga smiled, and Danny began to relax. If they couldn't be with their own mother, at least they were with people who seemed kind.

Suddenly someone shoved past Danny, and he stumbled, regaining his balance. "Hey!" Danny exclaimed.

But the heavyset man who had been responsible neither saw nor heard Danny. He had stomped across the lobby to face John Wilkes Booth. Danny couldn't hear what the two men were saying to each other, but anger had darkened their faces.

Olga edged close to Alfrid. "True gentlemen would remember their behavior while in a public place," she murmured.

Alfrid put a hand on her arm, and there was sadness in his voice as he said, "True gentlemen would not be so ready to divide our country."

An anxious-looking man in a gray coat rushed to intercede. Danny heard him say sternly, "Gentlemen! I must ask you to leave this hotel. You will have to continue your conversation outside." Booth and the man who had confronted him didn't answer. They simply turned toward the main doorway and strode from the lobby.

Olga shooed Danny and Peg toward the restaurant, but Danny carried with him the image of the terrible hatred that had twisted both men's faces and burned in their eyes.

3

THE SWENSONS' HOUSE was south of St. Joseph, on a rise high above the Missouri River. The low hills rolled to the west and north, the river gleamed beyond them, and thick woodland crowded to the south and east edges of the fields.

Danny's mouth fell open at the sight of the two-story house that rose, gleaming white, at the peak of the highest hill. At each side of the front porch were two tall decorative columns, and he could see a brick chimney rising from the shake roof at each end of the building.

Real fireplaces! Danny thought, hunching his shoulders in a happy hug. Back in New York City, he had sometimes paused in front of one of the elegant houses along the avenues to peer inside before someone saw him and closed the heavy draperies. On cold days, as he'd glimpsed the warm golden and orange flames, he'd wished he could know what it would be like to sit in front of a cozy fire and be truly warm. Now he would know!

The barn was large and to the south of the house, separated from the house only by a double width of the drive. As they neared the barn, and Alfrid pulled the horses to a halt, Danny could see the nearby privy and well beyond the house. Close to the barn was a chicken house, and behind it, dotting the edge of a recently harvested field, was a row of tall haystacks. The tingling smell of the sun-dried hay blended with the rich earthy fragrance from the meadows, and Danny breathed it in deeply.

Suddenly he caught sight of a vegetable garden. "A real garden!" Danny exclaimed. "I recognize the squash. I've seen squash like that in the markets."

Peg's eyes were wide as she stared where Danny was pointing. "Squash grows on the ground?" she asked. "With those big leaves?"

Danny poked her. "Where did you think it grew? On trees?"

Peg shrugged and thought a moment before she solemnly answered, "I've never had a single think about squash."

Olga giggled, lifted Peg over her lap, and handed her down to Alfrid. "You may help plant our next garden. Would you like to plant some squash?"

Peg ducked her head to hide her mischievous smile. "Oh, yes!" she said. "As long as I never have to eat it!" Olga took Peg's hand, and they laughed as they hurried toward the house.

Danny was a little shocked at Peg's ready laughter. Could Peg have forgotten Frances and Megan and Mike and Petey and Ma—especially Ma—so soon that she could be happy without them?

She's only seven, he reminded himself. *You do want her to be happy, don't you?* The answer that flashed into his mind was a grudging, *Yes. But not yet,* and he squirmed, uncomfortable with his own thoughts.

Quickly he jumped from the buggy, ready to follow Olga and Peg, but Alfrid put a hand on his shoulder. "Wouldn't you like to lend me a hand with the horses?"

"Oh! Y-yes, sir!" Danny stammered, embarrassed at appearing ignorant or—even worse—lazy.

Alfrid patted Danny's shoulder, then took a grip on the reins and clucked to the pair of matched brown horses, which were still hitched to the buggy. "You're not used to farm life yet," he said. "I would be just as lost and unknowing as you are right now if I were suddenly set down in New York City."

Danny followed behind the buggy, grateful for Alfrid's words of kindness. He *did* feel lost. How was he to know what he was supposed to say or do?

He kept his eyes on Alfrid. He liked the way the man walked with long, purposeful strides. Alfrid was not as muscular as Da had been, but he walked just as tall and straight, holding his head high. And he was kind, like Da, even though he didn't smile much.

Danny tried to reassure himself. *I probably don't need to worry any longer,* he thought. *Signs are that Alfrid will be a good foster father.*

At one side of the barn was a section for the buggy. On the other side were open stalls for the three cows, who turned to stare at Danny, and stalls with half doors for the two horses.

Danny let out a long whistle and exclaimed, "This is grand!"

Alfrid unhitched the horses from the buggy, slipped the harness from their heads, and held out the leads to Danny. "Suppose you hold Flash and Fury while I open their stalls and fork down some feed."

"F-flash and Fury?" Danny stammered. The horses

snorted, bobbing their heads, and one of them looked right into Danny's eyes.

"Don't let the names disturb you," Alfrid said. "They're well behaved, if treated firmly."

Danny reluctantly stepped forward to take the leads, looking up into the faces of the horses. Eager for their stalls and food, they were restless, blowing gusts of warm air through their noses. "Th-they're fine, big animals!" Danny said, and gulped as one of the horses leaned down to snort at him with a noise that seemed as loud as the engine on the train. Danny squeezed his eyes shut tightly but held his ground.

He thought he heard Alfrid chuckle, but when he looked over, Alfrid's face was as solemn as ever.

"I'll take them now, Danny," he said. "Just step back so they won't tread on your toes."

With relief Danny backed up until he could feel a solid post behind him. He watched Alfrid rub down the horses with rough sacking.

Soon Alfrid stepped from the last stall. "We'll let them enjoy their meal before we give them a full rub-down," he said. Pausing, he tilted his head and studied Danny. "You did a good job," he added.

Feeling much braver, Danny said, "I can't wait to tell Mike about the horses." The realization hit him like a blow: he wouldn't be seeing Mike to share the story with him. Tears burned his eyes.

"Come with me," Alfrid said quickly. "I'll show you around the barn and the yard. One of your chores will be to help me care for the animals. Tomorrow I'll teach you how to milk a cow."

"I'd like to milk a cow," Danny said. Thinking about the warm milk caused his empty stomach to rumble so loudly that Alfrid heard and turned sharply toward him.

"When is the last time you've eaten?" he asked. "A real meal, I mean?"

"This morning on the train," Danny said. "We had bread and apples and milk." The cookies at the hotel had been delicious, but Danny had been too keyed up, and too flustered by the elegant surroundings, to do more than nibble.

"Not enough to hold you for so long," Alfrid said. "Let's take our tour of the farm later. It's probably just about time for dinner."

As they entered the kitchen, Danny knew dinner would be no hurried catch-as-catch-can meal. He inhaled a blend of the light fragrances of cinnamon and sugar and the deep buttery richness of roasting chicken. His mouth watered, and he gave a little moan of pleasure.

The kitchen was large and warm and tidy, with rows of cooking tools hanging on the walls and a pine cupboard with dishes and copper pans arranged in rows on its shelves. Centered in the middle of one inside wall was a huge brick fireplace open both to the kitchen and a room beyond. Through it, beyond the metal grate and swinging arm that held a steaming teakettle, Danny could see the legs of a table and chairs in another room.

A red-cheeked woman, strands of brown hair plastered across her damp forehead, her hands swaddled in toweling, pulled a covered dish from a brick oven and turned toward them. She was as round as though she were stuffed with pillows, and her smile was comfortable. "So this fine young man is the Danny you were telling me about," she said.

Olga put her arm around Danny. "Yes," she answered. "Danny, I'd like you to meet one of our near neighbors, Mrs. Ennie Pratka, who was kind enough to come and prepare a meal for us."

"It was no trouble. Just a way of being neighborly," Mrs. Pratka insisted. She put down the pan and hugged Danny with such enthusiasm that he was nearly smothered. Suddenly released, he staggered back. He saw the mischievous twinkle in Peg's eyes and knew she'd received the same over-abundant greeting. But Danny's interest lay more in the steaming bowls and platters of food crowded onto the table than in Mrs. Pratka.

"Wash up! Be quick about it!" Mrs. Pratka cheerfully ordered.

Alfrid led Danny to a table in one corner on which were a large bowl, a pitcher of water, a folded towel, and a small bowl of soft lye soap. By the time they had washed their hands, Mrs. Pratka had lined up Olga and Peg behind her, Olga with a bowl of potatoes, Peg proudly carrying a bowl of applesauce.

"Alfrid, you carry the large platter of chicken, and Danny, you take the bowl of cream gravy," she said. "Mind you, it might be hot, so be careful not to drop it. I'll come back for the beaten biscuits."

Without question they all obeyed her, and Danny had the strange sensation of being part of a parade.

As they seated themselves, Danny leaned toward the platter of chicken, breathing in its deep fragrance. He closed his eyes, delighting in the moment, but Mrs. Pratka firmly set down the plate of biscuits, plopped into her chair, and said, "Napkins in your laps, children, and bow your heads while Mr. Swenson 'turns thanks."

"Turns *what*?" Peg asked.

"Returns thanks to God for all His bounty," Olga murmured, and smiled at Peg.

Danny willingly bowed his head, thankful, also, that Alfrid's prayer was short. His stomach rumbled loudly again, and he pressed his hands against it.

"Amen!" Mrs. Pratka said loudly, and without pausing for breath, added, "Fill up your plates, children. There's plenty for seconds and a good bread pudding for dessert."

Danny ate as he had never eaten before. Mrs. Pratka was a little bossy, but she made up for it by being a fine cook. One of the reasons Ma had sent the children west was so they'd have nourishing meals. Danny hoped that Frances and Petey and Megan and Mike were eating food this good.

He paused, a fork loaded with a large bite of gravy-smothered biscuit in his hand, suddenly unable to swallow. This wonderful food wasn't worth being parted from the people he loved. He'd give anything to be back home eating boiled cabbage with Ma and his brothers and sisters. Nothing could take their place.

"Danny? You don't like my biscuits?" Mrs. Pratka's voice brought him back to the present.

"Oh! Oh, yes, I do!" Danny stammered. He couldn't give in to tears. Not now. He took a deep breath and tried to smile as he said, "You're a fine cook, Mrs. Pratka." He quickly popped the bite on his fork into his mouth.

"Then have another biscuit," she said, putting one on his plate and generously spooning cream gravy over it. "Tyrus—my late husband, may he rest in peace—was always partial to my beaten biscuits."

Peg spoke up around a mouthful of food. "What happened to your husband?"

Olga gave a little warning frown to Peg. "I'm sorry, Ennie," she murmured.

But Mrs. Pratka shook her head impatiently and said, "It's a good question, and I don't mind answering." She leaned across the table to look directly at Peg and said, "Tyrus came down with the grippe, and it went into pneumonia, and he never got better."

"Like our Da," Peg said. "He was supposed to get better, but he didn't. I was scared and we all cried."

"Peg!" Danny muttered. "That's enough." With one fist he rubbed at the tears, which this time he'd been unable to fight back.

Mrs. Pratka shifted her attention to him. "It hurts a lot to lose someone you love," she said, "and there's no getting around it. But life goes on, and that's the way it is, so we may as well make the best of it."

Danny could hear Ma saying, "And that's the all of it." The same idea. It made sense, and in a way it was such simple, straightforward advice that it made him feel better. He put down his fork, noticing that the other plates were empty, too. "I'll clear the table," he said, and scrambled to his feet.

Olga rose from her chair. "Thank you, Danny, but there's no need," she said. "Mrs. Pratka and I can manage."

"But I want to help," Danny said.

Alfrid stood and reached for a bowl. "We'll all help," he said. "The more helping hands, the sooner we get to the bread pudding. Do you have cream for it, Olga?"

"Of course," she said. "There's a cooled pitcher down in the root cellar."

"Not anymore there isn't." Mrs. Pratka gave a hearty laugh. "It's on the kitchen worktable now. I borrowed just a little for the biscuits." Olga laughed with her.

Danny was surprised that neither of the Swensons seemed to mind Mrs. Pratka coming into their house and taking over. On the one hand, why should they mind when she cooked such a wonderful meal for them? But on the other, she dominated the conversation, and Danny was desperately curious about Olga and Alfrid. This was an entirely new life for him and for Peg, with a new home, new parents, and new ways of doing things. Frankly, he admitted to himself, this part was more frightening than helping Alfrid with the horses.

As he carried the last empty plate to the kitchen, Mrs. Pratka was still rattling on. "And oh, wasn't Tyrus the one to save every little thing." She pointed to a huge ball of twine on a shelf near the back door. "He would have greatly admired your thriftiness, Olga."

"What *is* that thing?" Peg asked, looking where Mrs. Pratka had pointed.

"Olga's one folly, but a harmless one," Alfrid said. He tenderly put an arm about his wife's shoulders.

Olga tossed her head, pretending to be miffed, but couldn't help smiling. "Don't make sport of me," she said. "It's just that I can't abide to throw away the good, sturdy pieces of twine that tie the feed sacks and purchases from the store. Who knows when they'll come in handy?"

"She ties them together," Alfrid explained to Danny and Peg, "and winds them into that ball. We expect it to grow bigger and bigger until it takes up the entire kitchen. Then we'll have to do our cooking out-of-doors."

"Oh, Alfrid," Olga said with a giggle. "Enough of your teasing. Who's going to dish up the bread pudding?"

By the time the meal was over, the kitchen cleaned, and they'd said their good-byes to Mrs. Pratka, Danny was so tired he could hardly keep his eyes open; but Olga gave Danny and Peg a tour of the house, and Alfrid showed them around the farm.

That evening the fireplace in the dining room was comforting, the flames casting shadows that jumped in and out of the dark corners of the room. Danny spooned in the hot beef soup Olga had served them, hoping he wouldn't fall sound asleep at the table. Even Peg's chatter had come to a halt.

Peg dropped her spoon with a clatter. "I'm so tired," she murmured.

"Of course you are, dear," Olga said, and immediately got up to help Peg from her chair. "I'll take you upstairs right now and tuck you into bed."

"Better take Danny, too," Alfrid said. "He's about ready to turn his soup plate into a pillow."

Danny pulled himself up in his chair. "I'll help with the dishes," he said.

"Not tonight," Alfrid said firmly. "It's up to bed with you. Your room is next to Peg's."

"Can't Danny sleep with me?" Peg asked. At home all the children had shared the same bed.

"From now on you and Danny will have your own rooms," Alfrid told her.

Peg's lower lip quivered. Alfrid picked her up and swung her to his shoulder. "She's overtired," he said to Olga. "She'll be asleep by the time her head touches the pillow."

Olga picked up a lamp and went ahead of them up the stairs. She lit the lamp in Danny's room, then kissed him softly on his forehead. "Good night, Danny. Sleep well," she said. "There's water in the basin so you can wash, and I've put your clothes into the chest. Your nightshirt is on top. If there's anything you need, please call us."

Danny nodded, glad when the door closed behind her. As quickly as he could manage, he pulled off his clothes, tugged on his nightshirt, and dove under the quilt on his bed. He'd save the washing up for some other time.

He heard footsteps going down the stairs and Alfrid's and Olga's voices murmuring together. Then in the silence, through the wall of his room, he heard Peg crying.

"Peg," he said. "Peg, can you hear me?"

There was a snuffling whimper and a creak of her bed before she answered, "Yes."

"Stop crying. It won't help. And you've got to go to sleep."

"But I'm lonely."

"You won't be if you're asleep." Danny's eyelids were so heavy they ached.

"Come and sleep with me, Danny," Peg begged.

"I can't. We're supposed to sleep in our own rooms."

20

Peg began to cry softly again. "I miss Ma," she moaned. "I miss Frances and Megan."

Danny struggled to sit up. "Be quiet," he said. "They'll hear you downstairs." He waited a minute, but Peg's sobs didn't stop.

"All right. I'm coming," he groaned and slid from the bed, wincing as his feet hit the cold plank floor.

Danny stealthily opened his door. There was enough light coming from the hall downstairs so that he could find his way to Peg's room. He opened the door and shut it just as quietly, stifling a cry as he stubbed his toe against the end of her bed.

Peg scrambled up to cling to him. "Get back in bed," he ordered. Danny squirmed from one position to another, trying to get comfortable on her bed. "I can't sleep here," he complained. "This bed's too narrow."

"Don't leave me," Peg insisted. "We can pull the quilt off the bed and sleep on the floor."

"Don't be silly," Danny said. "Here. I'll curl up next to your feet. Just don't kick." He tugged the bottom end of the quilt over him.

"I won't. I promise," Peg whispered.

"You always do," Danny mumbled.

"I do not," he heard Peg say. If she said anything else, he missed it as, with a sigh, he dropped immediately into sleep.

Later, mixed with the dreams that murmured through his mind, Danny felt a pair of strong arms lift him and pillow his head against a hard shoulder.

"Da?" he whispered. Danny could picture his father smiling, nestling his chin against Danny's curly hair. "Da," he said again.

"I'm here," a deep voice whispered. "Go to sleep. Everything's all right."

21

Danny could feel himself being tucked into bed, the quilt snuggled under his chin, and a rough hand stroking back the hair from his forehead. He heard the door shut and slid back into his dreams.

4

WHEN DANNY AWOKE, he was confused. His body still felt the constant jolting motion of the train, but he was in a warm bed, a quilt pulled up around his ears and sunlight streaming into his face. "Mike?" he mumbled and reached out for his brother.

His fingers bumped the chest hard enough to wake him. Now he remembered. Mr. and Mrs. Swenson. The drive to their farm. Peg crying in the night. Curling up to sleep at the foot of her bed.

But now he was in his own bed.

Danny could hear people moving and talking downstairs. Was Peg with them? As fast as he could, he clambered into his clothes, splashed his face and hands with cold water, and flung open his door. The door to Peg's room was open, and the bed was neatly made. *Oh, no!* Danny thought. He was the last one up!

He clattered down the stairs and ran into the kitchen, stopping short as Olga, Peg, and a tall skinny girl with blond hair and big eyes stared at him.

"Lazy, lazy stay-abed!" Peg chanted, but Olga smiled and held out a welcoming hand.

"You needed your sleep," she told Danny, "and now you need a good breakfast."

Peg jumped up and down. "I had an orange!" she shouted. "A *real* orange! And Gussie is going to bring me a kitten, a black one with white paws, and Mama combed my hair and she's going to make me a rag doll so I'll have company when I go to bed, and I'm going to name the kitten all by myself, and—"

From all Peg's prattling, one word had stood out, hitting Danny like a blow to the chest. "Peg!" he interrupted. "You called Mrs. Swenson *Mama.*"

Peg stopped, surprised. "That's what she said I could call her."

Danny could feel his face turn hot and red, but he couldn't stop. "We already *have* a Ma."

"I know that," Peg said. "Ma is our Ma, and Mrs. Swenson is our Mama. It's different, see?"

Olga put an arm around Danny's shoulders. "I didn't know it would upset you, Danny. We'll think of another name, something easier to say than *Mrs. Swenson.*"

Peg's lower lip drooped. "I like to call you *Mama,*" she insisted.

Danny looked Olga square in the eyes, took a deep breath, and said, "Sure, it's a good name. Peg should call you that if it pleases the both of you. It's just that it took me by surprise, and there's so much to get used to. I didn't mean to—to—"

Olga pulled him forward, at the same time giving his shoulder a reassuring pat. "You and Gussie haven't been introduced," she said. "Gussie comes in each day to do many of the household chores. She's a fine girl and a good help, and we feel very lucky to have her."

Gussie gave Danny a broad, lopsided grin. Danny guessed that she wasn't much older than fourteen, but her arms were hard and muscular, and as they shook hands, her grip was a strong as a man's. Danny tried not to wince as he pulled his hand away.

"I would have been here yesterday when you come," Gussie said, "but the widow Pratka chased me off soon as I'd cleaned all the vegetables for her. She said she'd do the rest of what needed to be done." Gussie's grin became even wider. "The widow Pratka likes to take charge of everything and everybody."

"Now Gussie," Olga said. "Ennie Pratka is a good, caring woman. She only wants to help."

"She needs another husband, 'stead of livin' with kinfolk. She needs a husband who'll do right for her and not die penniless, like Mr. Pratka done. That's what my ma says."

Olga's cheeks turned pink. "That's enough, Gussie. No more gossip. We all have work to do."

Gussie cheerfully picked up her bucket and rag, leaving the room as Olga turned to Danny. "Breakfast for you first," Olga said, "and then you might like to join Alfrid. By this time tomorrow you and Peg will be at school."

"School!" Danny's mouth fell open, and he could feel his heart hammering with excitement. "A real school? They told us we'd have schooling, but I—I didn't dare to think about it. Peg and me—we've never been to school before."

"Can you read, Danny?"

"Yes, ma'am. I like to read near as much as Mike does." He glanced down at Peg with concern. "But Peg's young. She never learned."

Peg's chin jutted out, and she made a face at Danny. "Mama said I don't need to know yet. She said that's what school is for, to teach people to read and know their letters and cipher. Bet you don't know all that, Danny."

As it happened, he did, but before he had a chance to answer, Peg went on. "Gussie's going to give me the dinner pail she used to carry. And she's got one for you that used to belong to her cousin who got work laying telegraph lines."

Peg chattered on, but Danny had stopped listening. As he wolfed down his orange along with eggs and biscuits and fried potatoes and ham, he tried to imagine what schooling would be like. He couldn't picture it. He had no idea what to expect.

All day he worked with Alfrid, starting to learn how to care for the horses, hearing with excitement the first splash of milk into the pail as he milked the cows, and walking the boundaries of the farm. But part of his thoughts kept racing ahead to the next day and school.

Finally, Alfrid led Danny to a clearing at the far western boundary of his property. At their feet the ground sloped away steeply. Open fields below them stretched out to the banks of the broad Missouri River.

"This is one of my favorite sights," Alfrid told him. "I like to see the twists and turns of the river. It's like a silver snake."

"It's like a snake with spots," Danny said. "Look at all the boats!"

Alfrid nodded. "There are almost as many boats as on the big Mississippi. You crossed it on your way here. Do you remember?"

"Oh, yes. That I do. We crossed on a ferry, a steam-driven side-wheeler," Danny said. "It was grand! One of the lads—Jim was his name—said he hoped to be chosen by a family who lived in a boat on the river."

"I doubt he'd have much chance for that," Alfrid said.

"That's just what Mike told him," Danny said. "Mike's smart. He always knows what's what."

Alfrid looked down at Danny. "I know that you're a smart boy, too. Has Olga told you that tomorrow you'll be going to school?"

"That she has," Danny said. He took a deep breath. "I want very much to go to school, but ..." He paused, furrowing his brow.

"But what?" Alfrid asked.

Danny tried to find the right words. "Of course, I know that school is for learning, but I don't know how it's done. Peg will be with the little ones, so it will be easy for her, but I don't know where to go, or where to sit, or what I should say. I want to do things the right way and not have other lads thinking I'm stupid."

"I understand," Alfrid said, nodding solemnly. "Fortunately, I can tell you what you need to know." He sat on the grass, and Danny dropped to a spot beside him. "The school is in a one-room building," he began. "Each morning the teacher will ring the school bell, as a sign that school has begun, and all the boys and girls will go into the schoolroom."

"And when I go into the room, where do I sit?" Danny asked.

"As to where your desk will be in the schoolroom, I don't know. The teacher will have to tell you," Alfrid said. "The girls sit on one side of the room, the boys on the other. The little children are in front, the older children at the back. You'll probably be somewhere between the middle and the back of the room."

Danny nodded. He figured that he could wait until the others were inside and see where the boys sat. "What should I do with my dinner pail?"

"There's a section of the room at the back that's called the cloakroom," Alfrid explained. "There are plenty of hooks where the boys and girls hang their coats, and there are shelves for the dinner pails." Danny nodded again, and Alfrid went on. "There's a stove in the center of the schoolroom, and desks around it. When this new school was opened a few years ago, each student had a desk, but now there are more families in the area, so I understand that many of the children have to share desks."

"You said the boys sit together, so at least I won't have to share a desk with any girl."

"Anything else?" Alfrid asked seriously.

"What's the teacher like? When I think about him, I imagine someone very important and smart who looks like Abraham Lincoln."

The corners of Alfrid's mouth twitched. "Miss Abigail Clark wouldn't appreciate being compared in looks with Abraham Lincoln," he said. "Miss Clark is a young woman who came from Illinois last year to take the position. She's well spoken of."

Danny sighed with relief. He'd been worried about that impressive teacher.

"Oh, yes. One more thing," Alfrid added. "Behind the school building there are two privies, one for boys and one for girls, and they're clearly marked."

"Ah," Danny said. He'd been too shy to ask, but this was exactly the kind of information that was good to know ahead of time.

"I think we've covered the situation nicely." Alfrid climbed to his feet. "I can't foresee any problems for you."

Danny was satisfied. He couldn't foresee any problems either. He couldn't wait until the next morning, when he'd be able to see it all for himself.

5

SINCE THE SCHOOL was only a mile and a half from the Swensons' home, Danny and Peg could walk there and back each day, but Alfrid escorted them on this first trip to show them the way. Peg's legs were short, so the walk took longer than Alfrid had anticipated, and when they arrived at the school yard, it was empty.

Danny could hear a murmur of voices reciting something in unison. "Will you go inside with us?" he asked Alfrid. Danny's palms were damp, his stomach hurt, and he wished that he didn't have to leave Alfrid. He wished that no one had ever thought of sending him to school.

"It will be better for you if I don't," Alfrid said. "You can show the other boys that you can stand on your own two feet."

As Alfrid turned and walked back down the road, Danny gulped, fighting down the fear that rose in a lump inside his throat. He wouldn't be sick. No! He couldn't be.

"Danny, are you scared?" Peg asked.

"No!" Danny snapped.

"Mama told me not to be scared," Peg said. "Mama told me that on my very first day at school I'd make a new friend. She told me I'd have lots of friends."

"Peg! Will you be quiet!" Danny felt close to tears. All the answers he'd gotten from Alfrid were useless against the awful panic he was feeling.

It was better to get this over with as soon as possible, Danny decided. They couldn't stay out here forever. He grabbed Peg's hand and strode toward the building.

"Danny, wait!" Peg wailed so loudly that Danny was sure everyone inside the schoolhouse had heard her.

Danny didn't pause. "Come on, Peg. We're late already!" he snapped.

The door opened with a loud creak and twenty or so students turned to stare.

The teacher, a young woman whose rosy face was framed with a coil of dark hair, smiled at Danny and Peg. "Please come in," she said. "Are you new students?"

"Yes, ma'am," Danny said.

Peg tugged at Danny's arm, and he struggled to keep his balance. "Danny!" she whispered loudly.

"I'm Miss Clark," the teacher said. "And what are your names?"

"I'm Danny Kelly, and this is my little sister, Peg," Danny said as Peg jerked on his arm again.

Miss Clark's forehead wrinkled as she thought. "I don't know of a Kelly family nearby," she said. "Where do you live?"

"Danny! Listen to me!" Peg insisted loudly.

Some of the boys were leaning from their desks to stare at him. A girl about his own age tossed back her curls and snickered.

"Be quiet," Danny growled at Peg. He hadn't thought about how he'd explain who they were. He tried to speak up but had to clear his throat and start again. "Our family's not here," he told Miss Clark. "Peg and I are living with—that is, we were adopted by— No, that's not exactly right." He took a deep breath. "We came west from New York City, and Mr. and Mrs. Swenson took us in."

"Oh!" Miss Clark beamed at them. "You're children from the orphan train!"

"Danny!" Peg pulled on his arm so hard that he lost his grip on his dinner pail, and it clattered to the floor. "I have to find the privy!" she shouted. "Right now!"

Some of the children broke into laughter, and Danny's face grew hot. But Miss Clark immediately pointed at one of the older girls and said, "Elsie, will you please take Peg to the privy? Peg, when you return you can sit in this front-row desk with Molly. Danny, please put your dinner pail and your sister's dinner pail and your coat back in the cloakroom. Then you can share a desk with Wilmer Jobes. Wilmer, raise your hand so that Danny can see who you are."

A boy raised his hand slowly and squinted at Danny. Wilmer had a thick shock of straight, tan-colored hair, a long, thin nose, and dark eyes set close together. Danny estimated that Wilmer and he were about the same size and probably about the same age. *I'll have to watch out for that one*, Danny decided.

Danny hung up his coat, and as he was approaching the desk, Wilmer suddenly thrust out a leg. But Danny was ready for it. Instead of tripping and sprawling in the aisle, as Wilmer obviously had hoped he would, Danny brought down his weight on Wilmer's toes.

Wilmer let out a smothered yelp and slid across the seat, as far from Danny as he could get. Danny sat down, took a deep breath, and looked up to see Miss Clark standing beside him, holding a book. "Do you read?" she asked.

31

"Yes, ma'am," Danny answered.

"Let's see how well, so I'll know where to place you," she answered. "Will you please turn to the story on page three? While the others are preparing their lessons, you may come to my desk and read to me." She turned to walk back to the front of the room.

Danny fumbled with wooden fingers against pages that seemed to stick together, forgetting for the moment about Wilmer, who took advantage of the situation by giving Danny such a shove that he toppled into the aisle.

Miss Clark turned at the sound of the thump and looked at Danny with surprise. Then she looked at Wilmer. "How did that happen, Wilmer?" she asked.

As Danny scrambled up, he glared at Wilmer, who was gazing at Miss Clark with wide, innocent eyes.

"I dunno," Wilmer said. "Maybe he's just clumsy."

"Danny?" Miss Clark turned to him.

"I guess that's right," Danny said. He muttered to Wilmer from the corner of his mouth, "I'll talk to you later."

"You and who else?" Wilmer whispered.

"Are you ready to read, Danny?" Miss Clark asked. "I'm waiting."

Aware of the impatience that had crept into her voice, Danny hurried to her desk and began to read aloud.

As he finished the story, Miss Clark smiled. "Very good, Danny. Thank you. You'll be with the group reading from the fifth reader. Boys and girls in this group, we'll all turn to page twenty-five, and I'll ask Elsie to read the first paragraph."

During the rest of the morning Danny tried to concentrate on his lessons, but he had to keep part of his attention on Wilmer, ready for whatever his desk mate would try next. To his surprise, however, aside from an occasional jab from a sharp left elbow, Wilmer ignored him.

Danny was surprised when Miss Clark pulled a round watch from her skirt pocket and announced that it was time for the noon meal. "You may eat outdoors today," she said. The students crowded to the cloakroom to get their dinner pails. Wilmer had been first, shooting from his seat as though starting a race. Danny wanted to make sure Peg was all right, and was happy to see her hand in hand with a little girl her size.

Danny was among the last to reach the cloakroom. He reached up for the two dinner pails—his and Peg's—and found only Peg's. But on the floor in the corner, against the wall, lay his dinner pail, the lid off and the contents spilled out. The package of sliced bread and cold meat was torn, and heel marks from heavy boots had stomped the food. Danny knew Wilmer had been responsible and he was furious.

He opened Peg's dinner pail. In addition to the wrapped package of bread and meat, she had an apple and a square of some kind of cake with a browned sugar crust. Fine. Now he knew what to look for.

He put the lid back on Peg's dinner pail just as she came into the cloakroom with her new friend. He handed it to her, picked up his own, along with the mess on the floor, and went outside.

Wilmer was sitting on a log bench with two other boys. When Danny appeared, they stiffened, alert, ready for trouble.

"Well, well, there's the boy from the orphan train, come here all the way from New York," one of them said.

"My pa said them Easterners are all abolitionists," the other boy said. "We don't need their kind in Missouri."

Wilmer simply kept his eyes on Danny and didn't speak.

Danny strolled toward them, smiled, and said, "Mind if I join you lads?" Before any of them could answer, he squeezed in next to Wilmer.

"Hey!" Wilmer spoke up. "Who invited you?"

In one speedy motion Danny reached over, grabbed Wilmer's dinner pail, and opened it. Inside, on top of the food Wilmer had brought, lay Danny's sugar cake and apple. "These are mine, so I'll just put them back where they belong," Danny said. He picked up the cake and apple and popped them into his own dinner pail.

"You can't—" Wilmer began, but Danny interrupted.

"Where did this mess come from?" he asked in mock surprise. "It couldn't be mine. It looks like the kind of slop *you'd* eat." He picked up the wad of torn and dirty bread and meat and slammed it into Wilmer's pail. He glared at Wilmer and said, "If you ever try anything like that again, I'll feed it to you bite by bite."

"I'd like to see you try it!" Wilmer snarled.

"Oh, would you now?" Danny said. As he put down his dinner pail, the other two boys quickly scurried out of the way.

Wilmer was faster than Danny had anticipated. He kicked Danny's feet out from under him, gave him a shove, and leapt up as Danny fell backward over the log. " 'Bite by bite,' was it?" Wilmer taunted.

Danny had tangled with some dirty fighters in New York City. Now that he knew what to expect, Wilmer's tricks would be nothing new. Danny stood, took off his coat, jumped over the log, and faced Wilmer.

They were evenly matched, Danny decided. Wilmer moved lightly and quickly, however, and Danny could see that kicking was one of his favorite moves. Wilmer had taken off his coat, too, throwing it to one side, and he stood with his right shoulder hunched, his arms up, his hands balled into fists.

Good, Danny thought. *The way he's holding his shoulder, I can tell that he's not as good with his fists as he is with his feet.*

"What's the matter, orphan boy?" Wilmer taunted. "Are you afraid?"

34

"I bet he thinks he'll get in trouble with the teacher," one of the other boys said, and laughed.

Danny hadn't given Miss Clark a thought. If he got into trouble—well, in this case he hadn't a choice.

"Maybe we should just shake hands and make up," Wilmer suddenly said. He took a step toward Danny and held out his right hand.

But Danny spied the glint in Wilmer's eyes and was ready. He took a step toward Wilmer as though he believed Wilmer were sincere, but when Wilmer's right foot shot out, Danny easily jumped aside.

With his right fist he clipped Wilmer so hard on the jaw that Wilmer sat down with a thud on the packed ground.

Some of the other children had begun to gather around them. "You're gonna get in trouble if you fight!" a girl warned.

"Want to shake hands now?" Danny asked and held out a hand to Wilmer.

"Yeah," Wilmer said and raised his right hand. "I do. Help me up first."

As Wilmer gripped his hand Danny knew he had made a mistake. Wilmer was strong enough to jerk Danny off his feet. The two of them landed in a heap in the dust.

Pummeling as hard as he could and smarting from the blows he took, Danny rolled over and over on the ground with Wilmer. He heard Peg's voice crying out, "Leave my brother alone!" and someone else shouting for Miss Clark.

All at once Danny felt himself grabbed by his shirt collar and the waistband of his trousers and hauled roughly to his feet. He was face-to-face with Tom, one of the older boys. Another boy—Charlie—had pulled Wilmer up and to one side. "It's over now. Forget it," Charlie said to the crowd that had gathered.

Tom ordered Danny and Wilmer, "Get yourselves

dusted off before Miss Clark gets out of the privy. Hurry up."

"Who started this?" Charlie asked. "You up to your old tricks, Wilmer?"

"He's an Easterner, an abolitionist," Wilmer said sullenly.

Charlie's eyes narrowed. "What's wrong with that?"

Wilmer looked startled, than wary. "Well, that wasn't exactly why we were fighting. Don't matter. The fight's over," he said.

But Charlie's face was stern, and he remained staring down at Wilmer. "Slavery's wrong," he said, "and fighting for it makes everything worse."

Wilmer stuck out his chin. "Who says so? Just you and your family. My pa says if it comes to war, you'll all be traitors to Missouri!"

"Your pa—" Charlie began, but Tom interrupted.

"Don't get into that now!" he hissed. "Here she comes!"

Danny saw Miss Clark hurrying toward them. He tried to smooth down his hair, tuck his shirt back into his trousers, and look innocent at the same time. He knew he hadn't succeeded when she stopped in front of him and asked, "Were you boys fighting?"

Wilmer shot a look at Danny, then rubbed the toe of one boot in the dust. Danny took a deep breath and said, "You might say we were getting acquainted."

Miss Clark's eyebrows rose. "By rolling around in the dust?"

"It could be that was the best way we could find out what each other is like."

He could see that Miss Clark was struggling to keep a straight face. "We don't allow fighting here at school, Danny."

"Yes, ma'am," he said.

"Do you understand that, Wilmer?"

"Yes," Wilmer answered. He glanced at Danny with a puzzled expression.

"Very well. Now that you both understand, you'd better finish your meal," she said. "And hurry up. It's almost time to start lessons again."

As Miss Clark walked back toward the schoolhouse, Wilmer said to Danny, "I thought you were going to tell her about your dinner pail."

"Well, I didn't," Danny said. "Besides, you would have just denied it, and your friends would have backed you up."

Wilmer nodded. "Maybe, but you don't know that for sure."

"Are you saying that you'd really tell Miss Clark that you stomped half my food and stole the rest?"

"That's over and done with, isn't it?"

"Not when my stomach is so hungry it's growling as loud as two dogs with one bone."

Wilmer shrugged. "My ma packed me too much food, as usual," he said. "If you want I could give you some corn bread and a slice of fatback."

"Thanks," Danny said.

As they walked back to the log and sat down, the other two boys joined them. "This here's Henry and that's Nat," Wilmer said, as the boys opened their dinner pails again. "They're brothers." He turned to Danny. "I'm like you. I ain't got any brothers, just sisters."

"I've got two brothers," Danny said, his mouth filled with corn bread.

"Where are they?" Nat asked.

"They got placed in other homes."

"Other homes? Hereabouts?"

Danny shook his head. "Petey's off in Kansas, and Mike's living on a farm somewhere in Missouri. I don't know when I'll see them again."

For a few moments the other boys were silent, and

Danny struggled to gulp down the lump that rose in his throat. Then Wilmer said, "I'd trade any or all of my sisters for a brother, but if I had a brother I wouldn't want him to go away." He took a large bite of molasses cake and added to Danny, "That's my sister, Gussie, who works for the Swensons."

Danny took a bite from his apple and sticky juice ran down his chin. He wiped it away with the back of one dusty hand. "I like Gussie," he said. "She's nice."

"She's bossy," Wilmer said. He licked molasses cake from each of his fingers, then rubbed his hand down the leg of his trousers. "All my sisters are bossy. My pa says someday they'll all grow up and get married and move away, but it's hard to wait that long."

The bell in the tower of the schoolhouse clanged loudly, and the boys and girls still in the yard grabbed up their things and hurried to get inside the building. As Danny finally slid into the desk next to Wilmer, Wilmer turned to him and gave him a conspiratorial smile.

"We're going to work hard on our spelling lesson," Miss Clark said, "because we have to get ready for the spelling bee."

"What's a spelling bee?" Danny heard Peg ask.

"It's a contest to find the best speller in the school," Miss Clark explained.

"I'm going to win," Wilmer whispered to Danny. "It'll be easy."

Danny grinned at him. "That's what you think." He'd take Wilmer on in any challenge!

"We'll have a box supper with your parents, and our entertainment will be the spelling bee," Miss Clark said. "It's a fall tradition." She rapped on her desk with her knuckles. "Pay attention, please. While I'm working with the younger children, you boys and girls from the third form up, take out your books and slates and get to work.

Danny, I have a slate you can borrow until you get one of your own."

The slate was passed to Danny, and he took it eagerly. He'd never used one before. He checked to see what Wilmer and the others around him were doing with theirs, then worked as they did, copying the spelling list in his reader, writing the words over and over again as he tried to remember the position of the letters. It wasn't hard. It was fun. So Wilmer thought he was going to win, did he! Wouldn't he be surprised when Danny came out way ahead of him!

When Danny and Peg arrived home late that afternoon, Gussie took one look at Danny and reached for a clean cloth. "You can't let Miz Swenson see you lookin' like that!" she said.

"Show me my kitten first!" Peg said, jumping up and down in excitement. "Where's my kitten?"

Gussie grinned at Peg. "In that box in the corner. Mind you pick him up gentle now."

"He's beautiful!" Peg squealed. "And look at his long whiskers! That's what I'm going to call him—Whiskers!"

As Peg knelt by the box and scooped up her kitten, Gussie wet the rag from the kitchen water pitcher and scrubbed so hard at Danny's face and ears that he yelped and tried to squirm away.

"First day of school, and you got into a fight," she said. "It looks as though you was rollin' around in the dirt."

"He was," Peg said, "and so was the other boy."

"And who was this other boy?" Gussie asked.

"It doesn't matter," Danny said quickly.

Peg's nose crinkled as she tried hard to remember. "I don't know his name," she said, and Danny let out a sigh of relief.

"Well, the two of you know better than that," Gussie said. She held Danny off and looked at him. "You'll do

39

for now," she said. "And no more fightin'. Keep that in mind."

"Yes, *ma'am*," Danny muttered. Wilmer was right, Danny thought. Gussie *was* bossy.

Gussie grinned. "It don't make me no never mind if you call me *ma'am*," she said. "I kinda like it. If you did it all the time, I might even start to put on airs. Now, the two of you go into the parlor nice and quiet like and say hello to Miz Swenson. She's lying' on the sofa."

Danny asked, "Is she sick?" and held his breath, waiting for the answer.

"She gets tired easy," Gussie said. "She has good days and bad days. This just happens to be a bad day."

"Is it because of us? Did we make her tired?" Danny was suddenly frightened.

"No," Gussie said. "In fact, every time she talks about you and Peg, she colors up and laughs. You're good for her. Maybe even better than the ground beef bones in wine that the doctor told her to take."

The same tonic the doctor had prescribed for Da! Danny shuddered.

"Our Da got sick," Peg said, "and he died." Her voice broke, and Danny realized that Peg was as fearful as he.

Gussie made a shooing motion. "No more talk like that."

Olga, propped up with pillows, greeted them with open arms. Peg ran to her, snuggling both Olga and the kitten, and Danny surprised himself by hesitantly kissing Olga on the forehead.

"Thank you, Danny," Olga murmured, and smiled at him with such pleasure that Danny jumped back, knowing from the heat in his face that he was blushing.

"I wrote to your mother today," Olga said. "I knew how anxious she'd be to get news about you. When we go to town we can mail the letter." She paused and

40

looked at Danny. "I think it would be nice if you wrote to her, too, and to your brothers and sisters. Don't you?"

Danny didn't think so, but he nodded.

"Where is the list of their addresses—the one Mr. MacNair gave you?" Olga asked him.

Danny shoved his hands into the pocket of his jacket. "It's got to be somewhere," he said.

"Look upstairs," Olga said. "You may have tucked it into the chest for safekeeping."

Danny couldn't remember putting the list anywhere, and he didn't want to spend the rest of the afternoon looking for it. It would be too hard to explain to Olga why he couldn't write the letters yet. "I'll look for the list later," he promised. "Right now I think I should go outside and find Mr. Swenson. Maybe I could lend him a hand."

"All right," Olga said with a smile. "I know how glad he'll be to see you."

Danny took off his school clothes, tried to shake the dust and dirt from them, and slipped into his heavier work clothes. He paused for a moment, wondering if he'd lost that list on purpose because he didn't want to write the letters. Writing would make it all final. He had to keep believing they'd be a family again, or it wouldn't come true.

The sun that shone through his bedroom window was already sinking into twilight. He didn't have time to look for the list. He'd do it after supper.

Danny was no sooner out the kitchen door than Alfrid shouted to him over near the woods. Danny raced to join him, arriving out of breath.

"How would you like to help me collect and tie small branches for kindling and stack them on this sled?" Alfrid asked. "While we're working you can tell me about school. Do you like your teacher?"

"She's nice," Danny panted, slowly catching his breath.

41

"She asked me to read and said 'Very good,' and she lent me a slate until I can get one of my own."

"I forgot about slates," Alfrid said. "We'll make out a list of things you and Peg will need and go into town on Saturday. Now, what about the other boys? Did you make friends?"

Danny stood, a cluster of stout twigs in his hand. "First, could you tell me about Mrs. Swenson?" He felt a chill down his backbone as he asked the question. "Gussie says that Mrs. Swenson tires easily, and you told us that she was—was—I forget the word."

"Fragile?" Alfrid asked softly.

"Yes. That's it. Is she very ill?"

Alfrid's face grew solemn, and he looked right into Danny's eyes. "Olga's heart has never been strong," he said. "She takes the medication the doctor has prescribed, and I make sure that she has the rest she needs." He paused. "There are flowers that grow like weeds in the sun, and not even a storm can beat them to the ground. Then there are other flowers with pale, delicate petals. They're often the most beautiful, but they must be sheltered and protected. Olga is like one of those special flowers. Do you understand?"

"Yes," Danny said. He thought at first he did, but as they worked, he realized that Alfrid had really not answered his question. The late sun was warm on their backs, but Danny shivered.

6

THAT NIGHT PEG went to bed peacefully, a rag doll in one hand, Whiskers in his box next to her trundle bed. In the night she cried out once for Ma, but Danny, stumbling through sleep to wakefulness, heard Olga's voice soothing and quickly comforting her.

It was Danny who cried, muffling his sobs under the quilt. He missed Ma. He missed Mike. He missed everyone so much it was like a terrible aching sore that burned in his chest. *We've got to get together again. We've got to,* Danny told himself. *I'll think as hard as I can until I work out a way.*

He fell asleep and dreamed that Mike was coming toward him. Danny ran to Mike, so happy that his heart was pounding loudly against his ribs, but Mike began to fade and disappear. "Mike! Don't go away!" Danny called out. "Mike! Where are you?"

"There, there," a deep voice answered, and a gentle

hand touched his shoulder. "It was just a bad dream, Danny. Everything's all right. Go back to sleep."

Danny reached up and grasped Alfrid's hand, holding it tightly. He'd tell Alfrid about Mike. Alfrid would help him find Mike.... Alfrid's hand was warm and strong and reassuring. Before he could tell Alfrid anything, Danny was once again asleep.

In the morning, when Danny came downstairs, Olga was preparing breakfast, bustling about the kitchen as though she'd never had a tired spell in her life. Danny sagged with relief. It had been foolish to be afraid.

"Did you find your list of addresses last night?" Olga asked him.

Danny guiltily shook his head. "Maybe it fell out of my pocket at school. I'll ask Miss Clark if anyone found it."

Olga patted his shoulder. "Don't worry, dear. If your list doesn't turn up before Saturday, Katherine Banks surely can get the addresses for you. I know that she or Andrew MacNair has a copy. In the meantime, you can write the letters so they'll be ready to mail."

But in that meantime there were many things to do, and Danny pushed the letters from his mind. The next few days fell into a comfortable routine. Danny woke early, helped with the milking, and walked to school with Peg. He began to make friends with the other boys but found himself spending most of his time with Wilmer, who, on the whole, wasn't a bad sort.

Danny practiced hard for the spelling bee, wishing Laura Lee hadn't chosen him to be her study partner. Laura Lee's mother brushed her hair each morning into long sausage curls and tied them up in a cluster with a white ribbon. The bow on the ribbon reminded Danny of a giant moth, and each time Laura Lee shook or nodded her head, causing the bow to flutter, Danny's first impulse was to swat it.

Laura Lee blinked her eyes and giggled when she looked at Danny, which made him uncomfortable. He wished there was someone he could ask why Laura Lee acted like that and how to make her stop it. He couldn't ask Gussie, because she'd only tease. He didn't need teasing. He needed answers. If Frances or Megan were around, they'd tell him.

He sighed as he thought about his sisters. It wasn't just for advice that he needed them near. They were family, and he desperately wanted to have his family together again.

But he wanted Alfrid and Olga, too. Olga was kind, and Alfrid—well, Alfrid really listened to what Danny had to say and seemed to care about it. He was strong and gentle, loving and firm, everything a father should be. Each afternoon Danny would rush home from school and into his work clothes to help Alfrid with whatever needed to be done. Danny loved the farm chores, but most of all he loved being with Alfrid.

Gussie teased him. "You're a regular tagalong. You stay right on the mister's heels the same way Whiskers follows Peg."

But Danny didn't mind what Gussie said. "Mr. Swenson needs me," he answered proudly, content because he knew it was true.

On Saturday morning, excited about the trip to St. Joseph, Danny woke up before daylight. It was hard to choke down his breakfast and even harder to wait for the others to get ready. He couldn't wait to see Katherine Banks, who owned a general store in town. She had been so kind to all the children who had traveled to St. Joe from New York.

As though she were reading his thoughts, Olga said,

"Don't forget now, Danny. While we're in town, ask Mrs. Banks for the addresses you need."

"I won't forget!" Danny answered.

"I'll give you some envelopes," she said. "Have you written all the letters?"

"The letters?" Danny gulped. "With all I was doing, they sort of slipped my mind." He turned to Olga, who was watching him. "Once I get the addresses, I'll sit down and write all the letters. I promise."

"I know you miss your brothers and sisters," Olga said. "I don't understand why you don't write to them."

Danny shrugged. He didn't know what to say. It wasn't that he didn't want to write, and he certainly hoped that the others would want to write to him. He'd like to tell Mike all about Alfrid and to let Frances and Megan know how gentle and kind Olga was. And Ma—he missed her more than she could know, and he wanted to tell her so, but putting words on paper was so final! If he wrote about his life on the Swensons' farm, once the words were written, they would make it all come true. The Kellys would be scattered, leading separate lives, and couldn't be back together again as a family. But they had to be together. Danny wouldn't allow himself to think for one minute that he couldn't someday make it happen. All he needed was to work out the right plan.

Alfrid came into the kitchen, tugging at his gloves and stamping his feet on the mat. "Everyone ready?" he asked. "The horses don't like waiting."

Neither did Danny. Letters forgotten, he made a dash for the buggy.

Alfrid hitched the buggy in front of Katherine's store. He held out a hand to help Olga down, but she paused, tilting her head up to peer over the crowd that had gathered near the corner. Danny stared, too. He couldn't see the men who were shouting, but he heard their voices yelling angry insults. The argument was over slavery, and it was getting louder. Someone in the crowd shoved someone else. Was there going to be a fight?

"Come quickly now," Alfrid said as he lifted Olga to the ground and reached for Peg. "Get inside the store."

Olga's eyes widened and her face became pale as she held tightly to her husband's arm. "Alfrid, last time we saw an argument on the street, one of the men had a gun, and someone was hurt."

"All the more reason to hurry," Alfrid said.

Suddenly a tall, muscular man on horseback plowed through the crowd, and people jumped back, scrambling out of the horse's path.

"It's Andrew!" Danny exclaimed. "Andrew MacNair!"

"This is a civilized town," Andrew shouted at the men. "Take your brawls somewhere else! Get out of here! Now!"

The crowd broke up, some of the men grumbling, some of them strolling off as though they'd already lost interest in what had happened.

A stocky, well-dressed man hurried toward them. He rushed up to Alfrid, stopping only to tip his broad-brimmed felt hat to Olga before his words tumbled out. "We're planning a series of meetings," he said. "Our only hope is to try to educate every citizen against slavery. We must convince them of what is right, or the entire country will surely be headed for a civil war."

"War?" Danny gasped.

But the man paid no attention to Danny. "Alfrid, you're a man who likes to have time to cogitate," he continued, "but we have little time. We've contacted that famous political lecturer, Ralph Waldo Emerson. He's agreed to come to St. Joe to address us, and we're lining up other speakers. Will you come to the meetings? We need your support!"

"You have it," Alfrid said. "I've never had even a moment of doubt that slavery was wrong."

"Good." The man let out a sigh. "We'll call a meeting soon. We'll meet in the assembly hall over near the wharves, and I'll let you know the date as soon as it's set."

With another quick nod to Olga, the man hurried on his way.

Olga spoke in a low voice. "Attending those meetings could be very dangerous, Alfrid."

"It would be even more dangerous to do nothing," Alfrid said. "We have no choice but to stand up for our convictions."

Danny looked back to the street, hoping to see Andrew, but he was now out of sight. Andrew had been brave to charge that crowd. Alfrid was brave, too, and Danny was proud of him. He moved a little closer to Alfrid."

"When are we going to see Katherine?" Peg asked.

"Right now," Alfrid said, and holding Olga's elbow gently, he led the way into Katherine's store.

It was a busy place. Clusters of people were gossiping about what had happened on the street and examining the goods for sale. A clerk was rapidly tying up packages behind the counter, and Katherine was measuring off yards of striped cotton ticking for one of her customers.

She stopped when she saw Danny and Peg, stooping to give them each a hug.

"I have a kitten!" Peg began, and went on to tell Katherine all her important news, winding up with, "And Danny lost the addresses for Mike and Megan and Fran—Frankie and Petey."

Katherine nodded reassuringly at Danny. "I've got them at home," she said. "I'll copy them for you, and the next time you're in town I'll have them here at the store for you. Will that be soon enough?"

"Oh, yes. That's plenty of time," Danny answered quickly, even though he had no idea when Olga and Alfrid would return to St. Joseph. "I saw Mr. MacNair," Danny added, wanting to change the subject. "He stopped some men from fighting out in the street."

"So I heard." Katherine sighed and glanced at Alfrid. "These are difficult times," she said.

"Mr. McNair's very brave," Danny said.

For some reason Katherine's cheeks grew pink. "Yes, he is," she said. She quickly changed the subject. "Don't let that argument you saw give you the wrong impression of St. Joseph. You'll usually find interesting things, not frightening ones, on our streets. A few days ago we had a traveling fiddler, and I heard from someone who had come north from Springfield that sometime in the near future we'll probably be paid a visit by a medicine show."

"What's a medicine show?" Peg asked.

Katherine explained. "Someone has bottled tonic to sell—something he claims will make people feel better. He sells it by taking it from town to town in a fancy painted wagon. It's important for him to attract a crowd so he can sell the tonic, so he puts on some kind of a show. Last year we had a medicine man with a monkey who could do tricks, and that drew a big crowd. Many people here had never seen a monkey before."

"I would like to see a monkey," Peg said. "What's a monkey?"

Olga laughed and said, "Come, children. We have shopping to do, and Katherine has customers waiting for her help. We'll talk about monkeys and medicine shows later."

"And have tea and cookies?" Peg asked hopefully.

But the shopping trip didn't last long. As soon as they had picked out their school supplies and Alfrid had replaced a broken saw with a new one, Olga suggested that they return home.

"The fright this morning has tired me greatly," she whispered to Alfrid.

But Danny heard and was worried. Olga's illness, the fighting in the street, the threat of war—there was too much to think about. Alfrid surprised Peg and Danny with paper twists of peppermint drops as they began their trip home, but this treat didn't begin to dispel Danny's terrible feeling of dread.

7

THE NEXT MORNING Olga was able to accompany them to church services. Afterward she spoke to the minister, praising his sermon and introducing Danny and Peg.

Danny was relieved that the minister hadn't seemed to notice he wasn't paying attention. It hadn't been the minister's fault. When they'd sat down in the pew, Danny had noticed that Olga's hands trembled. The skin on them was so transparent that he could see the faint blue lines underneath. Olga's hands had reminded Danny of Da's, and he'd frantically said his own prayers that Olga wouldn't be as ill as Da had been, that she'd soon be well again.

Danny was introduced to so many people he couldn't begin to remember their names. Mrs. Pratka gave him another smothering hug. He could never forget Mrs. Pratka.

He was surprised when Mrs. Pratka arrived at the Swensons' only a few minutes after they returned home. She took off her coat, looked around for a place to put her hat, and finally stuck it on top of the ball of twine, which had grown a little larger after the last visit to town.

As Mrs. Pratka tied a large white apron around her ample middle, she said, "I know that your girl, Gussie, is off today, and I know you've been feeling poorly, Olga, so you get yourself off to bed for a good rest, and I'll cook up a meal that will put some meat on your bones." Without pausing for breath she continued, "Danny, get out of your churchgoing clothes and lend me a hand with washing and peeling the vegetables."

Danny hurried to obey, and while he was scrubbing the dark soil from a bunch of carrots, Mrs. Pratka said, "Worrying doesn't do any good, Danny."

He looked up, startled, and she added, "Your forehead is full of worry wrinkles. That doesn't help Olga. Just show her a happy smile. That's the kind of help she needs."

"I want her to get better soon," Danny said.

"We all want her to," Mrs. Pratka said.

She looked so sympathetic that Danny blurted out, "What if—?" then couldn't finish the sentence.

Mrs. Pratka sighed and put down the pot she was holding. "Danny, you're old enough to understand that life can be pretty hard at times, but it has a lot of good moments, too. You just have to keep your mind on the good parts and struggle through the bad ones. You've traveled a rough road yourself, so you know what I'm talking about. Now, let's see some spunk. Put a smile on your face." She glanced at the carrot Danny was holding. "And scrape all the way to the tops of those carrots. When you're done, cut them in chunks. Not slices, but chunks. Understand?"

Danny understood. He understood all of it. But he didn't want his life to have any bad times. He only wanted the good. He wished he could talk to Mike about the way he felt, or to Ma. He wished he could hear what Ma would have to say.

The days passed quickly, and the air grew chill. Each Wednesday evening Alfrid rode to St. Joe to attend the abolitionists' meetings.

"I'd like to go, too," Danny told him.

"When Ralph Waldo Emerson comes to speak, I'll take you with me," Alfrid promised. "I understand that the man is a fine orator."

"When will he come?" Danny asked.

"The date hasn't been set," Alfrid said. "You'll have to be patient."

But it was hard for Danny to be patient.

Mike wrote an excited, happy letter from his new home with Captain Taylor at Fort Leavenworth, and Frances wrote about how happy she and Petey were with their family. "I can be a girl again," she wrote. Danny smiled as he recalled how he'd last seen Frances: her hair cropped raggedy short, wearing a boy's trousers, all to keep her promise to Ma to try and stay with Petey. Ma wrote of her new job as a housemaid and her tidy little attic room in the fine house.

Danny read their letters over and over until the papers split at the folds, but he wouldn't allow himself to picture Ma's room and the house and the people in it, all of which Ma had described so well. He wouldn't let himself think about the fort and the soldiers and travelers who came and went. And he closed his mind to the Kansas farm that Frances wrote about. He had to keep believing that his family would someday be together again.

All anyone could talk about at school was the upcoming presidential election, even though every day Miss Clark reminded them to study harder to prepare for the spelling bee, Danny wondered if Miss Clark thought the spelling bee was more important than the election.

As the important Saturday evening drew close, they had to polish their desks until the wood gleamed. The day before the spelling bee, they carried in the benches Mr. Otis Palmer brought over in his wagon, so there'd be places for everyone to sit. Miss Clark scrubbed the floor, put a bowl of autumn leaves on her desk, and cautioned all her students to be very sure to be on time with their families the next evening.

Olga packed a large basket of food and tied a festive red ribbon on the handle. The color was mirrored on her cheeks, and her eyes sparkled with excitement.

"I used to be very good at spelling bees," she said. "I still remember the fun. Danny, you're going to do so well! And we're all so proud of you!"

It wasn't until they arrived at the schoolroom and Danny saw the crowd that had come that he began to get nervous.

Everyone dove into the box suppers first, most of the families sharing extra cake or fruit with one another. Danny wished they could have eaten after the spelling bee was over and not before. He found it impossible to choke down a bite.

Olga winked and whispered to him, "I've got some dinner set aside for you to enjoy later. There's a big piece of sponge cake tucked into this napkin."

Danny gulped. "I wanted to win the spelling bee, but now I know I'm going to lose."

"That's what all the contestants are thinking at this moment, isn't it?"

Surprised, Danny glanced around the room. Wilmer was fidgeting, drumming his heels against the floor, and one of his sisters was poking him, insisting that he stop. Charlie, Tom, Bessie—none of the participants in the spelling bee looked particularly happy. Well, then, he wasn't alone. The tight knot in his chest released a little.

In a short time napkins were folded over the baskets, which were then slipped under the benches. Ever since he had made and donated the benches, years ago, Otis Palmer had been the one who called out the spelling words. With an air of importance, he sat at Miss Clark's desk and opened the spelling book. The fifteen participants immediately hurried to their places in the line across the front of the room. Wilmer stepped on Danny's right foot, and Danny elbowed Wilmer in the ribs. "I'm gonna beat you," Wilmer whispered, and Danny just grinned, because he knew that would irritate Wilmer more than anything else.

The audience became quiet, and a whimpering baby was gently hushed. Mr. Palmer fixed Bessie, who stood at the end of the row, with a gaze so steady that she flinched. In rolling tones he called out the first word, repeating it with the same deliberation: "Amicably. Am-icably."

"Am-amicably," Bessie stammered. She closed her eyes and took a deep breath, then recited, "A-m-a—"

"Wrong!" Before Bessie could open her eyes, Mr. Palmer said, "Next. Spell *amicably.*"

Bessie stumbled to a seat against the wall, her face flushed with embarrassment. The very first word, and she'd missed it! Danny felt so sorry for Bessie it was all he could do to keep from groaning aloud. What if he missed a word, too?

It dawned on him that Charlie, Bessie's partner, had spelled the word correctly, and Mr. Palmer had shot out another word to Tom, the next in line. "Neighbor," Mr. Palmer was saying.

Danny's knees wobbled. Thank goodness someone else was getting that word! Tom spelled it correctly, and

Mr. Palmer went on to Alice May, who left the *e* out of *pursued* and was dropped from the competition.

Laura Lee spelled *pursued* correctly, and suddenly it was Danny's turn. "Weigh," Mr. Palmer said.

Danny's mouth fell open. No! Not that word! He couldn't go down on his first word, and for the life of him he couldn't remember how to spell it. The *i* and the *e* were the same as in *neighbor*. What had Tom said?

"Weigh," Mr. Palmer repeated in his voice that reminded Danny of church bells tolling at a funeral.

Danny knew that he had to say something before time ran out. He took a deep breath and closed his eyes. "Weigh," he said. "W-e-i-g-h."

He had actually taken a step out of line before he realized that Mr. Palmer had gone on to Callie June with the word *partisan*, so he must have spelled his word correctly. With a long sigh he leaned against the wall. The worst was over.

As each round passed, and the words became harder, more of the contestants had to drop out. Soon they were down to ten, then eight, and Danny was still in.

So was Wilmer.

Mr. Palmer looked at Laura Lee. "Farinaceous," he said.

"Huh?" Danny muttered under his breath. He didn't remember ever seeing that word.

Apparently Laura Lee didn't either, because she got completely tangled in the vowels. "Wrong," Mr. Palmer boomed, and Laura Lee flounced to her seat.

His gaze bored into Danny's skull. "Farinaceous," he said.

"Farinaceous," Danny repeated. "Uh ... uh ... f-a-i-r—"

"Wrong," Mr. Palmer said.

Head down, Danny walked to the bench where the Swensons sat. Olga squeezed over and made a place for him. "That was a dreadful word," she whispered. "I never would have got that one right."

Danny glanced at her, surprised to see that she was smiling. "We're so proud of you!" she said. "Look how well you did! There aren't many left in the competition."

Danny looked to the front of the room, where only the older students, Tom, Charlie, Annie, and Elizabeth, remained standing.

"Where's Wilmer?" he whispered.

Alfrid leaned to whisper in return, "He went down on the same word you did."

So! Wilmer had missed it, too! The tight place in Danny's stomach immediately disappeared, and he realized how hungry he was. He could hardly wait until the spelling bee was over so he could eat.

But the last four contestants were top-notch spellers, and the match continued. Finally Tom and Annie went down on *pernicious*. Soon afterward Charlie missed *vertiginous*. Elizabeth, with a gleam of triumph in her eyes, spelled the word correctly. She was declared the winner, and a wide blue ribbon was pinned to her shirtwaist.

"I'm satisfied," a loud voice could be heard all over the room. "Don't even mind my own not winnin', long as that boy from the abolitionist family didn't take the match."

There was silence for a few seconds, as everyone turned to stare at the man who had spoken, Wilmer's father.

Miss Clark made little shooing motions, as though she were trying to clear the room, and called out, "Thank you for coming, everyone! I hope you'll all be at our Christmas pageant! December twenty-second. Don't forget! Thank you, thank you."

But one of the other fathers, a muscular, red-faced man who spoke with a thick German accent, had stepped up to face Wilmer's father. "You're a hothead and a troublemaker, Jobes," the man said. "What are you trying to do? Start a war right here and now?"

"I got a right to speak my piece," Mr. Jobes said.

"Not here in a schoolroom. Not among peaceable people."

People around Danny began pushing forward, and he could hear muttering.

Alfrid leapt to the bench, where he towered over the others like a strong tree in a forest. "Everyone outside, right this minute!" he demanded in a loud voice. "The spelling bee is over. Harvey Greenwood, you're nearest to the door. Please open it wide so that everyone can leave this room!"

Mr. Greenwood did, letting in a blast of cold night air. Shivering people began struggling into their coats and snatching up their baskets.

Danny was amazed. Alfrid had done the same thing that Andrew had done. Both men had given strong orders, and people had obeyed. Did most people want someone to tell them what to do?

The school yard was soon cleared of buggies and wagons. Olga rested against Alfrid on the way home, her head on his shoulder. "Oh, Alfrid, how will it all end?" Danny heard her murmur.

"For the best, I hope," Alfrid answered.

They rode in silence for a few minutes until Alfrid spoke in a hearty voice. "Danny did us proud tonight. This is a time to celebrate."

"I didn't win," Danny said.

"You came very close," Alfrid said, "which is all the more amazing because you've had no formal schooling up until now."

"He studied very hard," Olga said proudly.

"I'm sure he did," Alfrid said, "but I think the real answer is that Danny's own mother and father were good teachers."

"Yes, sir. They were," Danny said, his heart so filled with love for Alfrid that he wished he could leap up from his seat in the buggy and throw his arms around him.

When Alfrid went into town to cast his vote for Abraham Lincoln in the presidential election, he took the rest of the family with him. "This is an important moment," Alfrid said to Danny as he guided his buggy through the crowded streets. "I want you to remember it always."

Danny nodded. "Yes, sir!" he said, excited about the crowds, the banners hung on poles, the street-corner orators, the band in the city square, and the festive air in St. Joseph.

They left the horses and buggy in the livery stable and walked toward the courthouse. Danny stopped in front of a wide open door to watch a blacksmith who was heating metal in a forge, the muscles on his bare arms glowing red-gold with sweat. He was a wide-shouldered, handsome man with a shock of black hair. When he looked up to see Danny watching him, he smiled.

Alfrid, who had come back to see why Danny was lagging, waved and called, "Good day to you, John." Then he turned to Danny, saying, "Come along. The others are waiting. We'll watch John Murphy at work some other time."

Olga had packed a generous picnic lunch. Although the air was nippy, the day was bright, and there was room in the park to spread a quilt on the ground for a picnic.

Peg was the first to spot the high, brightly painted wagon at the north end of the park. "Is that a medicine man? Do you think he has a monkey?" she asked.

Alfrid took her hand. "Let's take a look," he said. "We may enjoy a show before we eat."

He led the way, Olga and Danny following. They

joined a small crowd gathered around the open end of the wagon, on which bottles of tonic and pills were displayed. A gentleman wearing a black frock coat and tall silk hat raised his right hand, and a small bouquet of brightly colored paper flowers suddenly appeared in it. People in the crowd gasped and applauded.

Danny gasped, too, but for a different reason.

"A magic show!" Peg shouted, as Alfrid swung her to his shoulders for a better view.

The magician turned and smiled at Peg, and Danny had a good look at him. Heavy, dark eyebrows and beard, a large nose and ruddy cheeks. Danny knew that face. He tugged at Alfrid's arm. "I have to talk to you," he whispered.

"Can you wait just a minute, Danny?" Alfrid asked.

"No," Danny said. "It's important."

The man had now displayed an oversize pack of brightly painted playing cards. Although two or three women in the audience murmured their disapproval at the sight of playing cards, which suggested wicked pastimes, no one left. Others joined them, and the crowd grew larger.

Alfrid turned Peg over to Olga and walked to one side of the group, bending down to hear what Danny had to say.

"I know that man," Danny said. "He calls himself Dr. Claudius Mundy, but he's not a real doctor."

"How do you know?" Alfrid asked.

"He used to live in New York City. I saw him, and Mike told me ..."

The memory was vivid in Danny's mind—the two of them craning their necks to find out what the crowd was watching. Mike knew everything and everyone on the New York streets. "See that man?" he had said in a low voice. "That's Mundy. He's running a shell game—he'll get all those people's money."

Danny had watched, fascinated, as the man deftly scooped up a pile of coins. "He's the worst kind of snake-oil merchant, too," Mike went on. "Sells stuff in a bottle that's supposed to cure people, but you can bet it only makes them worse. Some doctor."

Now, looking into Alfrid's concerned face, Danny told him the rest. "Later Mike found out—and he told me—that Mundy's medicine really did kill somebody, and that the police were after him but he'd disappeared."

Dr. Mundy had finished his magic act and had begun talking about the wonderful curative powers of the tonic he had for sale.

"I learned the secret formula from an Indian medicine man," Mundy was saying. "It's full of rare herbs that will cure neuralgia and pleurisy and do wonders for the rheumatiz." A few people edged forward to buy bottles of the tonic.

Alfrid thought a moment, then said, "Maybe we should find out what's in those bottles."

He strode through the crowd until he reached the side of the wagon, Danny following in his wake. Alfrid picked up the nearest bottle and held it up to the light, peering through the dark green glass.

"That tonic costs fifty cents, mister," Dr. Mundy said. "Pay up before you help yourself." He laughed, and a few people standing nearby smiled.

"I'm only looking," Alfrid said.

Dr. Mundy frowned. "Pay up, or put it down," he demanded.

Danny saw the muscles in Alfrid's jaw tighten, and Alfrid took a firmer grip on the neck of the bottle. "What's that residue at the bottom?" Alfrid asked.

"Residue?" For a moment Dr. Mundy looked flabbergasted, but he quickly regained his poise. "Why, that's the secret Indian herbs what will make folks feel healthy and energetic again, once they drink it." He turned to the

61

crowd. "A spoonful a day, folks. Best tonic you've ever tried. A real cure-all."

"It looks like river sediment to me," Alfrid said, "Missouri River mud."

Dr. Mundy growled a curse and tried to snatch the bottle Alfrid was holding, but Alfrid pulled some coins from the watch pocket in his coat and slapped them down on the gate of the wagon. He deliberately unscrewed the cap of the bottle and held it under his nose.

"Ugh!" Alfrid said. "This is river water that has stood too long. It stinks of slime and scum!"

A few people nearby exchanged murmured comments, and a hand that was holding out some coins quickly pulled back.

"You're scum yourself! Get out of here!" Mundy hissed at Alfrid. "You got no call to interfere with my business."

"And you've got no right to try to poison people," Alfrid said.

One of the men in the crowd elbowed forward with an opened bottle. "This isn't tonic! What are you trying to get away with?"

"Give us back our money!" a woman shouted.

Dr. Mundy, his face dark red with anger, struggled to stay in control. He raised his voice and said firmly, "No need to shove or shout. If you're not happy, I'll refund your money. Folks know my good reputation wherever I go."

"Not in New York," Danny said. "Your tonic killed a man there."

"A lie! The boy is lying!" Dr. Mundy shouted, glaring at Danny.

"I am not lying," Danny said. "You aren't a real doctor, either."

"The man's a crook!" someone yelled.

"A cheat! Give back our money!"

62

A woman screamed as the crowd pushed toward the wagon.

Dr. Mundy handed back coins as fast as he could, tossed bottles of pills and tonic helter-skelter into the wagon, and scrambled to lift and lock the wagon's gate. He paused in front of Danny, grabbing the collar of his coat and poking his face close to Danny's. "I won't forget you, brat!" he said. "I'll get you for this."

Alfrid roughly shoved Dr. Mundy aside. "Get out of this town and don't come back!" he warned.

"I'm going!" Dr. Mundy untied his horse's reins and jumped to the seat of his wagon. "But I'll be back!" he snarled. "You can count on it!"

"Don't be afraid of him," Alfrid said to Danny as they watched Mundy's wagon rattle down the street. "He's known in St. Joe now. He won't want to come back."

But Danny suspected that for once, Dr. Claudius Mundy was telling the truth.

8

THE NEWS FINALLY arrived by telegraph that Abraham Lincoln had been elected president of the United States.

"When the Southern Democrats split from the Northern Democrats, dividing their vote, it allowed the Republicans to win the election," Alfrid explained. "In St. Joe, Lincoln got 410 votes out of the 452 votes cast!"

Danny was delighted. He was sure that now everything would begin to change for the better.

But it didn't. The people who had worried that war might be possible were now positive that war was inevitable. Word came that raids along the southern Missouri–Kansas border had increased in violence. Men had been shot and their farms burned. On the streets of St. Joseph there were heated discussions about secession.

During this turmoil Danny accompanied Alfrid on his trip to town to purchase supplies. He leaned from the wagon to peer at a group of men who had crowded around a speaker and were interrupting his speech with enthusiastic shouts and cheers.

"I wonder what they're so excited about," Danny said. "I wish I could hear what the man is telling them."

Alfrid glanced at the group and sighed. "I know some of the men in that group. I'm afraid they're Southern sympathizers. The speaker is probably trying to raise money for the Southern cause. Unfortunately, he'll probably be successful."

People in the crowd shifted, some of them contributing to a hat that was being passed around. Danny sucked in his breath as he thought he spied a familiar face. "Mundy! He came back!" Danny cried.

Alfrid drew the horses to a halt and craned to study the faces in the crowd. "I don't see him, Danny," he said. "Can you point him out to me?"

As the crowd began to disperse, Danny tried to spot Mundy again, but he finally shook his head. "I don't see him now. Maybe he went down that side street."

"I think you must have made a mistake," Alfrid told him. "It's hard to believe that the man would return to St. Joe. I honestly don't think you have anything to fear from Mundy."

But Danny did fear Mundy. It was hard to get the man's twisted, angry face out of his mind.

Every day at school there were arguments between the abolitionists and the antiabolitionists. One afternoon the hostile feelings erupted into an uncontrollable fist fight involving every boy over the age of nine and a few of the older girls.

Miss Clark rushed frantically around the schoolroom, trying to separate the fighters, but she couldn't be everywhere at once.

Wilmer's fist collided so hard with Danny's right cheek that he staggered backward. Danny gasped with shock and shouted at Wilmer, "I thought we were friends!"

His whole body shaking in anger, Wilmer spat back,

"We can't never be friends! Not as long as you and your family are dirty abolitionists!"

Danny, sobbing with hurt and fury, flung himself at Wilmer.

In spite of Miss Clark's tearful efforts, the blows didn't end until the fighters were too exhausted to continue. Surveying the array of blackened eyes, bleeding cuts and scrapes, and torn clothing, Miss Clark announced that, as a suitable punishment, there would be no Christmas pageant.

Peg cried all the way home and into the parlor, flinging herself into Olga's arms. "I was going to be an angel!" she wailed. "And now I can't, and it's Abraham Lincoln's fault!"

"It is not!" Danny shouted at her. "It's the fault of the stupid people who believe in slavery!"

Gussie roughly grabbed his shoulder and jerked him back. "Look at you!" she said. "You come in the house all dirty, with your eye puffed out to here, and your clothes torn and bloodied, and then go blamin' other folk. For shame!"

Peg continued to sniffle, and Gussie immediately turned on her. "Take your tears somewhere else, Missy. Miz Swenson don't need to hear all your troubles. The two of you—look how you've upset her!"

Peg pulled back, her red-rimmed eyes wide with concern and guilt. "I'm sorry, Mama," she whispered to Olga.

"Dear little love, it's all right," Olga answered. "Part of being your mama is listening to your problems and trying to help." She attempted to rise from the sofa on which she'd been lying. "I'm worried about the swelling around Danny's eye. I'll wash his face and—"

Gussie interrupted her. "You just lie back, Miz Swenson," she said. "I'll tend to Danny."

Olga obediently sank back against the pillows. Danny

was shocked to see how weak she was. She seemed to have lost more weight, and a thin blue line throbbed in her neck. Why hadn't he noticed? There'd been so much to think about, so much to do.

"I didn't mean to upset you," he told Olga. "I won't get into a fight again. I promise."

"I promise, too," Peg echoed, her lower lip wobbling.

"There's no harm done," Olga said and smiled at them. But as they followed Gussie from the room, Danny turned to glance at Olga and saw her sigh and close her eyes.

Tears rolled down his cheeks as he sat in the kitchen and let Gussie wash the dirt from his face and swab at the scraped place on his chin.

"Don't be such a baby," Gussie grunted. "It don't hurt that much."

"It's not that," Danny said. "I was remembering Da when he was so sick. And Mrs. Swenson—"

"Hush!" Gussie whispered, and gave a jerk of her head in Peg's direction. But Peg was huddled on the floor in front of the fireplace, cradling her cat, her face buried in Whiskers's fur.

Gussie was right. He should help Peg, not make her feel worse. Danny gulped back the tears and said, "Peg, don't feel bad that we won't have a school Christmas pageant. You can sing your angel song to Mr. and Mrs. Swenson and Gussie and me."

Peg raised her head and looked at him mournfully. "It's not the same," she said.

"It'll be better," he told her, "because you'll be the only one performing. We'll all be watching you."

He could see Peg thinking about this, and she sat up a little straighter.

"Wait till you taste the good Christmas food," Gussie said. She wrung out the cloth and handed Danny a linen towel to dry his face. "Everybody makes steamed Christmas puddings with lots of fruit and nuts and suet and spices, and serves them hot with a big lump of hard sauce on top."

"What's hard sauce?" Danny became interested in spite of himself.

Gussie smiled and rubbed her stomach. "It's butter and sugar beaten together. When it's put on the pudding it melts and runs down the sides." She sighed. "It's the best-tastin' stuff you'll ever eat, not even exceptin' flummery."

"What's flum'ry?" Peg asked.

Gussie laughed. "It's a boiled custard. Talkin' of Christmas, tell you what let's do. Why don't we make Miz Swenson a sweet sachet for a Christmas present?" Peg looked so puzzled that Gussie added. "You two don't know nothin', do you? A sweet sachet's a packet of good-smellin' berries and leaves and such to lay in the wardrobe or chest of drawers, so all the clothes will smell good. Come on, Peg, let's see if we can find a bit of cheesecloth and ribbon to start with."

Danny ran up the stairs to change his clothes. He didn't want to think about Christmas. It would be his first Christmas away from Ma and Mike and the others, and he didn't know how he was going to stand it. Before the tears started again, he pulled on his coat and ran outside to find Alfrid.

As Christmas approached, the church was decorated with fragrant pine boughs, and the Swensons' house was warm with sugary, spicy smells. Fresh ginger cakes or crisp sugar cookies were waiting for Danny and Peg when they came in the door from school each day. Sometimes they'd eat them with cups of hot cider, warming their cold fingers against the mugs. Olga would smile at their pleasure in the treat. She looked more frail than ever and spent more and more time resting.

The winter gusts of snow and sleet brought most of the farm work to a standstill and brought Alfrid indoors, where he hovered near Olga. He made one trip into St. Joseph, traveling alone, and he came back with a solemn face, shaking his head at what he'd heard and seen in town.

"There's talk that when the Southern states secede from the Union, Missouri will go with them," he said. "Governor Jackson is urging secession."

Danny hadn't forgotten Dr. Mundy, and he had to ask. "Did you see Dr. Mundy?"

Alfrid shook his head. "I kept an eye out, but no sight of him. You must have been mistaken when you thought you saw him."

Danny hoped Alfrid was right. He never wanted to meet up with Mundy again.

Alfrid had brought letters to Danny and Peg from Ma and Megan.

"Megan wrote this herself!" Danny said to Peg. "She's learned to read and write!"

"When are you going to write to the others in your family?" Alfrid asked him.

"Danny!" Olga exclaimed. "You haven't written to your mother or brothers and sisters yet?"

Danny knew how stricken he must look, because Alfrid quickly said, "I didn't mean to get you in trouble, Danny, but Olga is right. Your family will want to hear from you."

"I'll write to them today," Danny mumbled. "Or maybe tomorrow, because I'll need to help with the animals, and then there's supper, and schoolwork to finish."

"Alfrid will excuse you from working out-of-doors," Olga said firmly. "You may write your letters now."

"Yes, ma'am," Danny said meekly. He followed Alfrid to the dining room and took a chair at the table as Alfrid lit an oil lamp against the afternoon's early darkness.

69

Alfrid placed on the table a bottle of ink, some sheets of paper, and a box containing penholders, tips, and wipers.

"Dear Ma," Danny wrote on the first page as soon as Alfrid had left the room. He stopped and stared at the paper through blurred eyes, and his stomach hurt. Ma was so far away, and she shouldn't be. She and her children should be together. He wanted to tell Ma that, but he couldn't. What could he write? He couldn't write anything that would make this all final.

Gussie came into the room carrying a stack of plates. "How are you coming?" she asked. "I'll need the table soon to set up for supper."

"I don't know what to write to my mother," Danny blurted out.

Gussie shrugged. "Don't ask me. I never writ to anybody in my whole life. Just think of somethin' pretty soon because in about half an hour we got to eat."

As she left him alone, Danny quickly wrote, "Peg and I are fine. How are you? Your loving son, Daniel James Kelly."

He leaned back and gave a long sigh of relief. That was noncommittal enough. He'd write the same to Mike, Megan, and Frances and Petey. Oh! And one more thing. At the bottom of the page he added, "Merry Christmas to us all."

Christmas was not merry in the Swenson home, in spite of the wonderful gifts Alfrid had made: a sled for Danny and a doll bed for Peg's rag doll. There was an orange apiece, some taffy candy, new clothes, and a roast goose dinner, cooked by Mrs. Pratka, ending with the spicy steamed pudding that Gussie had promised. But Olga had barely enough strength to attend the Christmas services at church, and as soon as the family arrived home, she took to her bed.

The doctor came the next day, but this time he talked

to Alfrid a long while, and when he left the house his face was solemn. Alfrid spoke to Mrs. Pratka, and Danny heard the few words which frightened him so much that he huddled in a corner of the parlor, his arms wrapped around his knees. Olga was going to die.

When Alfrid found him there, Danny clung to him, and he felt Alfrid's tears against his own cheek. All he could do was share Alfrid's sorrow. There was nothing he could say to Alfrid to help him.

But there was a great deal Mrs. Pratka could say. She was at the house every day, maintaining a constant chatter as she kept Danny and Peg busy with chores which Danny sometimes suspected she made up from moment to moment. She shepherded them in to see Olga when she felt that Olga was strong enough to visit with them for a few minutes, and she cared for Olga as tenderly as though Olga were her own kin.

"The widow Pratka is a hard one to work for," Gussie mumbled grudgingly, "but I give her this much. She's gettin' everythin' done what needs to get done."

Peg hugged her cat, but Whiskers was little comfort for her. Peg followed Danny around, snuggling up beside him whenever he had time to sit down. "When will Mama get better?" she kept asking.

"Peg, she's awfully sick," Danny answered the first time. "She might not—" But he stopped when he saw the terror on Peg's face. He hugged his little sister, and lamely finished, "I don't know. I just don't know."

It was the last day of December when Olga called for Danny and Peg to be brought to her room. Gently she kissed them and whispered, "I love you."

"I love you, too, Mama," Peg said.

Danny was so choked up he couldn't talk. He knew that Olga was saying good-bye.

Mrs. Pratka carried Peg off to the kitchen for milk

and cake and listened to her prattle, but Danny went upstairs. He rolled into a ball on top of his bed and cried until he fell asleep.

Sometime later Danny felt Alfrid scoop him up and hold him on his lap. Hearing voices in the hallway, Danny realized that Olga had died. "It isn't fair!" he cried. He hugged Alfrid tightly and sobbed, "You'll send us away now, and I'll lose you, too. You're my father, and I love you, and I need you, and now I'll lose you, just like I lost Da, and I can't! I can't lose you, too!"

"Hush," Alfrid murmured against Danny's hair until Danny had quieted, his sobs turning to dry shudders that shook his body.

"Listen to me, Danny," Alfrid said, his voice as soft as the darkness in the room. "I will not send you away. Your home is here with me. Eight years ago Olga and I had the heartbreak of losing our two sons to diphtheria. You are as dear as another son to me, and I have no intention of losing you as well."

"Promise!" Danny whispered.

"I promise," Alfrid said, and Danny heard him add, "Somehow, we'll work out a way."

9

"LIFE GOES ON," Mrs. Pratka said, and somehow it did, the ragged, tearing edge of pain slowly diffusing into a dull, spreading ache.

Alfrid's second cousin, Melba Wallace, came to stay for a while. She was a short, gray-haired woman who repeatedly sighed as she worked, like a miniature engine letting off puffs of steam. Although she was pleasant enough to Danny and Peg and told them to call her "Aunt Melba," she tended to talk about and around them as though they weren't there.

Mrs. Wallace seemed to get along nicely, however, with Mrs. Pratka, who came over nearly every day to help and often stayed to cook supper. Sometimes, when Danny and Peg arrived home from school, the two women would be bent over their needlework in a conspiratorial buzz of conversation.

Mrs. Pratka would boost Peg onto her lap and snuggle her as she asked about school.

At first Peg missed Olga so much that she couldn't eat and cried "Mama" in her sleep. Danny, who would creep into her room to hush and soothe her, began to worry that Peg would get sick, too, so he was thankful when she began to respond to Mrs. Pratka's attentions. On the day he heard Peg begin to chatter with the women, recounting a story with a laugh, Danny leaned against the door, sighing with relief. Peg was going to be all right.

Mrs. Pratka was kind to Danny, too, surprising him sometimes with hot cocoa and ginger cookies. Danny would gulp the treats as fast as he could and hurry outside to find Alfrid. He felt comforted and secure only when he was with Alfrid.

"In the early spring, before the planting, I'll have to hire a farmhand," Alfrid told him.

"I'll work hard. I can do what any farmhand could do," Danny said.

"Schooling comes first," Alfrid said.

"I can do both," Danny insisted. He wanted to prove to Alfrid that he was needed. And he loved Alfrid so much there was nothing in the world he'd rather do than work beside him.

The next few Sundays, after church services, Alfrid would leave Melba, Peg, and Danny for a few minutes to visit Olga's grave and tenderly lay a small holly branch or pine bough on the snow.

On the third Sunday Danny walked through the little cemetery with Alfrid, sorrowing with him, angry and fearful because there was no way he could help.

Alfrid laid a sprig of holly bright with red berries at the base of the headstone and murmured, "There'll be flowers in the spring." He stepped back and held Danny's hand firmly, but Danny knew that Alfrid wasn't talking to him; he was talking to Olga.

Then the last Sunday in January, as they drove home after services, Melba turned to Alfrid and said, "There's never enough time for mourning, Alfrid, but it's time you began thinking about taking another wife."

He gave her a sharp, quizzical glance before she added, "You can't run the farm by yourself. It takes two to make a go of it—a man and a woman. I can only stay a few more weeks to tend to you and the children. My own family needs me."

Danny sucked in his breath. Beside him Peg clutched at his hand, her fingers inside the wool mittens twisted into his so tightly it was painful.

"I don't want to think or talk of that now," Alfrid said.

Melba sat up primly, pulling her shawl more snugly about her neck against the cold air. "You had love in your marriage, which makes you more fortunate than many. But now you need a good, strong, thrifty woman who knows how to manage a household."

"Melba, this is no time to—"

"How do you expect to keep the children without a wife to aid you?"

Peg whimpered, then choked back the sound, staring at Alfrid with wide, frightened eyes. Danny's chest began to ache, and he found it hard to breathe.

"I'm not ready. There is no one—" Alfrid began, but Melba wouldn't give up.

"Yes, there is," she said. "Ennie Pratka is fond of you, Alfrid. She's a hard worker and would make a good wife."

"Ennie Pratka!" Alfrid's heavily gloved hands almost dropped the reins, and his mouth fell open.

"Think about it, Alfrid. That's all I'm asking. I know how stubborn you can be and how you have to mull an idea over and over before you'll accept it, but you're going to have to make a decision soon."

An idea exploded into Danny's mind with such force that he jumped. *That's it! Of course!* he thought. Peg gaped at him, and he leaned close and whispered in her ear, "Don't worry. I know what to do. I just thought of a wonderful plan!"

As the buggy stopped in front of the barn, Danny leapt out and ran through the snow to open the big barn doors. The moment that Alfrid led the horses inside, Danny unhitched them and led them into their stalls. He waited until the horses had been rubbed down, then turned to face Alfrid. "I don't think you should marry Mrs. Pratka," he blurted out.

Alfrid looked embarrassed. "Danny, Melba shouldn't have spoken in front of you and Peg. This is a matter that only I can decide."

"But I can help you!" Danny said eagerly.

"Help me?" Alfrid shook his head and hung the harness with the rest of the tack. "If you are going to try to assure me that you and Peg can run the house—"

"No!" Danny said. "That's not it. I understand that a man can't take care of a farm by himself. I just don't want you to marry Mrs. Pratka. I know someone else who'd make you a better wife. She's a grand woman who's a hard worker and strong as a whole team of horses. She'd make you a lot happier than Mrs. Pratka would. She'd make us *all* happy."

For a moment Alfrid just stared at Danny. Then he found his voice and asked, "Who is this woman?"

Danny smiled and answered, "Our mother."

"That would be impossible," Alfrid said.

"No, it wouldn't!" Danny spoke rapidly, intent on convincing Alfrid. "Ma can do anything, and do it well, and she's not afraid of hard work. She's used to it. Sometimes she sings while she works, and her voice is better than any you've ever heard in church. She has a ready laugh and a fine Irish wit, and her hair is as red as Peg's. Da used to tell her she was beautiful. And she is."

He took a deep breath, desperately groping for the right words to say. "Peg and I—it would be the best thing in the world if we could have Ma back again. But it isn't just for us. When the idea came to me I knew I had to tell you about it, because our ma would make you a good wife, a much better wife than Mrs. Pratka could be."

Alfrid sat hunched over on a nearby bale of hay and leaned his elbows on his thighs. "Your mother lives a long distance away, in New York City."

"But she'd come if we asked her and if you paid her railway fare! I know she would."

"To marry a man she's never met?"

"You're our father. I'd write and tell her what a fine man you are. We could ask Mrs. Banks and Mr. MacNair to write, too."

"The fare probably would cost a great deal of money."

"Maybe Ma has some saved, and I could try to get a job. You could ask Mr. MacNair what it would cost."

Alfrid rested his forehead in his hands. "That's enough for now, Danny. Sooner or later I must face the situation and give it some serious thought, I know, but it's been such a short time since we lost Olga."

Danny had been trying to help Alfrid, but he'd made him feel worse. "I'm sorry, Father," Danny whispered. "I love you."

With a groan, Alfrid lifted his head and enfolded Danny in a hug. "And I love you, son. I'll do whatever is best for us. I promise you."

Danny heard the kitchen door bang open and Melba calling, "Alfrid! Danny! What's keeping you? Ennie is here and wants to set dinner on the table!"

Alfrid stood, his hand on Danny's shoulder as they

walked to the open barn door. "We're coming," he called. "We're ready."

Danny guessed that Melba had told Mrs. Pratka about the discussion in the buggy, because Mrs. Pratka's eyes sparkled brilliantly, and she smiled broadly each time she looked at Alfrid.

"Ennie, your escalloped squash is wonderful!" Melba said. "And your chicken couldn't be better. Oh, if I could only make gravy like yours."

Mrs. Pratka dimpled and patted at her hair. "Tyrus—may he rest in peace—often said if they gave out medals for cooking, I'd be awarded a solid gold one."

"And he was right," Melba agreed. "A fine wife and a fine cook. No man could ask for anything more."

They both looked pointedly at Alfrid, who dropped his eyes and shifted in his chair.

Melba sighed dramatically and said, "Your stitchery puts anyone's to shame, Ennie. You're a woman of many talents. Don't you agree, Alfrid?"

Alfrid mumbled something. His face turned red, and he poked at his chicken with his fork.

It wasn't fair, Danny thought. Alfrid had said he needed time to think, but they were ganging up on him. What if the two women talked Alfrid into marrying Mrs. Pratka before he had a chance to consider Ma? Danny quickly broke into the conversation. "Can you sing?" he asked Mrs. Pratka.

She blinked with surprise. "What do you mean, can I sing?"

"I mean it's nice to hear someone singing around the house. Our ma liked to sing for us," Danny said. "Isn't that right, Peg?"

Peg put down her fork and her forehead wrinkled in a puzzled frown. "Yes," she said slowly. "She did. I almost forgot."

Danny stared at Peg in shock. "You forgot?"

"I said I *almost* forgot." Peg's lower lip curled out defensively, and her eyes swam with tears. "I wouldn't forget Ma."

Danny leaned back in his chair, suddenly without an appetite. He had counted on Peg to help him to convince Alfrid. But if she had grown so far away from Ma that it was hard for her to remember, she wouldn't be much use.

Melba shot Danny a quizzical look, then turned to Alfrid and said, "Before I leave I'm going to make an inventory of the pantry and see what you need to replenish it. Ennie has kindly offered to work with me. She's very quick and skilled at tasks like that."

"I'm glad to be of help," Mrs. Pratka said modestly.

"She'll need to know where everything is."

The way Mrs. Pratka simpered at Alfrid made Danny want to groan aloud.

"And there are some things that need to be disposed of," Melba continued, "like that foolish ball of twine on the back shelf."

"Leave that twine alone!"

"My goodness, Alfrid. I only suggested that—"

Alfrid's chair squeaked back, and he rose from the table. "Please excuse me," he said. "I have an important errand in town."

"But you haven't finished dinner!" Mrs. Pratka said. "And I made molasses pie especially for you because I know that you like it."

"Thank you," Alfrid said. "If you save a piece, I'll eat it for supper tonight."

"How about a nice big wedge now *and* one later? Sit down, Alfrid. I'll dish it right up."

She was halfway out of her chair when Alfrid said, "No! I'm sorry, but there is someone in town I must talk to."

79

"Who? And why must you go before you've finished your dinner?" Melba asked.

Alfrid didn't answer the question. He just said, "I should be home before dark. Danny, will you take care of the cows?"

"Of course I will," Danny said. "What else do you want me to do?"

"Just lend a hand to your Aunt Melba, if there's anything she needs."

"I will," Danny said.

No one spoke as Alfrid left the room. Danny could hear him in the kitchen pulling on his coat and boots. Then the kitchen door opened and shut.

Melba and Mrs. Pratka looked at each other. "What was that all about?" Mrs. Pratka asked.

"I don't know," Melba said. She turned to Danny. "Do you know what Alfrid's errand could be?"

"No," Danny said, trying to figure out the answer. "Unless it's a meeting of the abolitionists."

"Not on Sunday afternoon," Melba answered. "I wonder what Alfrid is up to."

Danny wondered, too. Alfrid had said there was someone he had to talk to. If it didn't have to do with the abolitionists, then who could this person be? Katherine Banks lived in St. Joseph. So did Andrew MacNair, when he wasn't scouting towns or off in New York with another group of Orphan Train children. Could Alfrid be going to talk to one of them? About Ma? About asking her to come to Missouri to be his wife?

Danny was wishing so hard for this to be true that he didn't hear when Mrs. Pratka spoke to him.

"Danny. Danny, what *is* the matter with you? You haven't finished your dinner either."

Danny opened his eyes and sat upright. "Please excuse me," he said, following Alfrid's example. "I'm not hungry, and I have to take care of the cows."

Melba just sighed and shrugged, raising her hands, so Danny scooted his chair back from the table.

"What happened? Was it the chicken? Was it over-cooked?" Danny heard Mrs. Pratka ask in bewilderment as he tugged on his coat, hat, and gloves and ran from the house.

He grabbed a shovel, throwing all his energy into cleaning the animals' stalls, working until he was per-spiring and panting, his breath rising in puffs of steam. Maybe, just maybe, Alfrid was asking Andrew about Ma and how to go about sending for her!

Danny paused, resting on the shovel. What would Andrew tell him? What if he advised Alfrid just to marry Mrs. Pratka? What if the railway fare from New York cost too much?

As another horrible thought struck him, Danny sagged against the side of one of the stalls, his knees suddenly wobbly. *What if Alfrid writes to Ma and asks her to marry him, but Ma won't come?*

10

By the time Alfrid arrived back at the farm, it was already dark, and Mrs. Pratka had gone home. Melba was so irritated with Alfrid that she had snapped at Peg and Danny all afternoon, and Peg had clung to Danny for comfort.

"What are you writing?" Peg had asked Danny, squeezing into the chair beside him and jostling his elbow. A drop of ink splatted one edge of the paper.

Danny had been too excited to care. "I'm writing a long letter to Ma," he had said. "I've got a lot to tell her."

"What?"

"I told her about—about Alfrid, and about the farm, and about how much we miss her, and I wrote what I told Alfrid about her, and ..." Danny looked carefully at Peg, wondering just how much information to give her. He decided to be cautious. "And I asked her to come and visit us."

Peg had gasped, jumping to her feet. "Could Ma do that?"

"Hush!" Danny had hissed at her. "This is our secret. Don't say anything until—well, until I tell you that you can."

Peg had nodded solemnly, her eyes shining.

Danny had quickly finished his letter and had taken it upstairs for safekeeping. He could mail it the moment Alfrid decided to send for Ma.

Now, as Danny heard Alfrid ride up, it was all he could do to keep from rushing to the barn to ask if he'd really gone to St. Joseph to talk to Katherine or Andrew. Instinctively, he knew he shouldn't. He had given Alfrid the idea, and he couldn't push him. Look what had happened when Melba and Mrs. Pratka had tried it.

Danny held his breath as Alfrid entered the parlor. Peg ran for a kiss, and Melba let out a long, aggrieved sigh. "Well," she said, "did you accomplish your very important errand?"

"Yes, I did," Alfrid said. He sat on the sofa next to Danny.

Melba's nose tilted a little higher and she sniffed. "Is it too much to ask that you tell me why you had to rush off as you did? You hurt Ennie's feelings. She thought you didn't like the way she had roasted the chicken."

"I'm sorry. I didn't mean to hurt anyone."

"You might tell her that."

"I will when I have the opportunity."

Melba sighed again and picked up her needlework. Danny gritted his teeth. He, too, was yearning to know why Alfrid had ridden into St. Joseph.

The room was silent for a few moments. Then Melba dropped the needlework onto her lap and looked directly into Alfrid's eyes. "Have you given any serious thought to our conversation this morning?"

"Yes, I have," Alfrid said. "I've decided you are right. I should make plans to marry soon."

Peg stared at Alfrid, hugging Whiskers so tightly that he mewed in complaint and tried to squirm from her arms. Danny closed his eyes, unable to breathe.

But Melba exclaimed, "Good! Ennie will be so pleased! I'll stay for the wedding."

"There may be a wedding, but it will not include Ennie," Alfrid said. As Melba's mouth fell open, he added, "I received the information I needed today from Andrew MacNair, and together we drafted a telegram in which I invited a woman to consider becoming my wife."

Melba shrieked, "You did *what*? Who is she?"

Alfrid rested a hand on Danny's shoulder. "Noreen Kelly," he said. "The children's mother."

Peg and Danny made such a racket, jumping up and down, hugging each other and Alfrid, and screaming with delight, that they didn't notice for a few moments that Melba had fallen back, swooning, into her chair. She had to be helped to her room, where she could loosen her corset strings and lie on her bed with a cold, wet cloth on her forehead, before Danny could question Alfrid further.

"Remember, your mother may not accept," Alfrid warned Peg and Danny. "She may not want to make a drastic change from life in the city to farm life."

"She lived on a farm in Ireland!" Danny said. "I'm sure she won't want to stay in a small attic room in New York, working for some other family, when she could be living in the countryside in a house of her own." He paused. "And with her own children again."

"Danny wrote a letter to Ma and asked her to come!" Peg said.

Danny ducked his head, then grinned at Alfrid. "Just in case that's what you wanted. It's ready to mail."

"Then we'll mail it tomorrow."

Danny hugged Alfrid. "You won't be sorry," he said.

"I hadn't planned to tell you until we had received an answer from your mother," Alfrid said. He glanced toward the stairs, and Danny knew what Alfrid meant when he added, "But things were rapidly getting out of hand."

"Who's going to tell Mrs. Pratka?" Danny asked.

He and Alfrid looked at each other. "Let's hope that Melba will," Alfrid mumbled.

A voice spoke from the doorway. "I will, and I'll add that you've taken leave of your senses," Melba said. She flounced into the room and sat stiffly on one of the chairs. "It's time for some plain talk, Alfrid," she said. "You don't know this woman you offered marriage to. You know nothing about her."

"Her name is Noreen Kelly," Alfrid said.

"All right. Noreen Kelly. What do you know about her?"

"Andrew said he was told she is a woman of great courage and principle."

Peg spoke up. "She's beautiful."

"She loves us," Danny said.

"She's our mother." Peg's face was shining.

Melba sighed and sank back in the chair. "Oh, very well, Alfrid. You were thinking of the children. But how can you—? You don't love this woman."

"You are the one who reminded me that love was unnecessary."

"But I didn't mean—" Melba broke off, frowning for a moment before she sat upright again. "What's done is done," she said. "Even though I think you've made a terrible mistake, Alfrid, now it's time to make plans for the future. When do you think you'll hear from this woman?" Alfrid's eyebrows dipped into a scowl, and she quickly amended, "Noreen Kelly, that is."

85

"We hope within a week or two."

"If she agrees, then she should arrive within another two weeks. Is that right?"

"I suppose so."

"Where will she stay when she arrives in St. Joseph?"

"Katherine Banks has offered her home."

Melba nodded, and Danny could see her ticking points off in her mind as though they were written on a long list. "Very well. The wedding can take place soon afterward. I will write to Samuel and tell him not to expect me until the latter part of February. In the meantime we will clean this house from top to bottom. I will not have Mrs. Kelly thinking that I shirked my job when I came to help you."

Melba, who was now caught up in her plans, rattled on, but Danny stopped listening. *Ma*, he thought over and over, as though his thoughts could reach her. *Ma, you've got to agree! You've got to come!*

The answer came by telegraph, much sooner than Danny had expected, and was hand delivered by Andrew late one afternoon. The icicles on the eaves outside the kitchen window had caught the sunlight, casting streaks of glittering, unnatural light into the room.

Danny felt as though he'd been caught in an unreal world, a sparkling kind of dream, as he watched Alfrid slowly and deliberately tear open the envelope, remove the message, and read it. So scared that his stomach hurt, Danny wanted to grab the paper from Alfrid's hands and read for himself what it said.

Peg stared up at Alfrid, while Melba and Gussie, who had been scrubbing out the oven in the brick fireplace, turned from their work. No one spoke. No one moved.

Finally Alfrid looked down at Danny and Peg. He began to speak, then had to stop and clear his throat. He

86

tried again, the muscles in his neck strained and tense. "Your mother will come," he managed to say.

Peg flew into Danny's arms, hopping up and down so excitedly that he had to fight to keep his balance. But he saw Alfrid turn to Andrew with a stricken look on his face and murmur under his breath, "What have I done?"

"Look at the children," Andrew answered.

Gussie got to her feet, dusting off her apron with hands so grimy they left black streaks. "Miz Kelly won't be the first wife sent for by mail," she said. "I heard about a whole boat full of 'em who sailed from New England all the way around to Oregon, because there was no women livin' there, only men badly needin' wives."

"Gussie!" Melba hissed. "Topics like that are not fit for a girl your age to speak of, especially in mixed company."

Gussie simply shrugged. "If you say so," she answered, "but it's a good story. If you want to hear it, we'll wait till the mixed company's gone outside and I'll tell you."

Andrew smiled and said, "Time for me to head back to town. It gets mighty cold once the sun goes down." Alfrid pulled on a coat and followed him out the kitchen door. Danny was right on their heels.

"My parents only knew each other two weeks before they were married," Andrew said. "Pa spied this pretty girl in town, asked her father's permission to court her, my mother was agreeable and of an age to marry, so that was that. They raised a family, were good to their children and to each other. I'd say it worked out well."

"But your parents were young," Alfrid said. "Mrs. Kelly and I have reached middle age. We've both been married before."

"That should make it all the easier for you to settle into married life again, shouldn't it?"

"I suppose so," Alfrid said. "I guess we'll just have to wait and see if it works out."

Of course it's going to work out! Danny thought. *It has to!*

As Andrew swung up onto his horse, Alfrid said wryly, "It's just occurred to me that for a man who has never married, you are pretty free with your advice. Perhaps I'd take what you say more seriously if you were married yourself."

"Maybe Mr. MacNair needs Aunt Melba to talk to him," Danny offered. "And to Kath—Mrs. Banks, too."

Andrew laughed, but his face flushed red. "Is it that obvious?" he mumbled, either to Alfrid or to himself. Danny couldn't tell.

Alfrid put a hand on Danny's shoulder. "That's enough, Danny," he said. "Mr. MacNair's thoughts are his own, unless he decides to share them with—with someone else." His eyes twinkled as he looked at Andrew, who flushed again, wheeled his horse, and rode off toward St. Joe.

Danny hoped to keep it a secret that Ma was coming, but with Gussie to report the story to Wilmer, there was no chance.

"I've heard the good news, Danny," Miss Clark said to him as he arrived at school, stomping the snow from his boots and tugging off his gloves to blow on his cold fingers. "I'm delighted that you'll be reunited with your mother!"

"I think it's exciting!" Laura Lee giggled and tossed back her curls. "Coming all that way to marry a man she's never met! I never before heard of anybody doing that!"

"Then you ain't heard of Zeke Moffat," Wilmer said. "Zeke farms that place down by the junction, and two years ago he got hisself a mail-order bride."

"Ma's not a mail-order bride!" Danny yelled at Wilmer.

"Your foster pa writ a letter for her, didn't he?"

"It wasn't a letter! It was a telegram!"

"Which makes it entirely different," Miss Clark said quickly. "I'm going to ring the bell in two minutes. Hang up your coats and get to your desks, and no more dawdling."

Danny managed to elbow Wilmer as they crowded into the cloakroom, but to his surprise, Wilmer didn't react. He hung up his coat, then quietly said to Danny, "I'm real glad that you're gonna see your ma again."

"Thanks," Danny said. He choked up and tears burned his eyes, but Wilmer pretended not to notice.

There'd be three weeks to wait, close to four, and Danny wondered how he'd manage to live through them. Each time he thought he'd explode with impatience he'd say over and over to himself, *Ma's coming. She's on her way. Ma will be here soon.*

The train that brought Noreen Kelly to St. Joseph arrived ahead of schedule, so she was waiting on the platform when Danny, Peg, and Alfrid arrived. Danny saw Ma standing tall and stately, wearing a deep blue full-skirted coat and a small blue feathered hat which set off her hair, causing it to gleam like fire in the morning light.

He and Peg raced to their mother, flinging their arms around her, and she dropped to her knees, tightly hugging them both.

"My darlin' Peg!" Ma cried. "Danny! Oh, love, how you've grown!"

With the laughter and hugs and kisses and even a few tears of happiness, Danny was heedless of the broad-shouldered, dark-haired man standing next to Ma until

89

the man helped her to her feet, saying, "You have a fine family, Mrs. Kelly."

Danny quickly looked up. He knew the man. His name was John Murphy, and he owned the blacksmith shop next to the stables.

"Good day to you, Danny," John Murphy said, his words musical with the familiar brogue. He glanced at Ma and smiled. "It was my great fortune to become acquainted with your mother soon after I boarded the train in Hannibal."

"Mr. Murphy's from Ireland, too," Ma said as she dusted off her coat. "Before he came to St. Joseph to live, Mr. Murphy lived in a town not far from where I was born." She smiled, too, looking not at Danny but at Mr. Murphy.

Danny frantically looked around for Alfrid, who had hung back, obviously wanting to give Danny and Peg the chance to greet their mother without interruption. But this was no time to hang back. It was time for Ma to stop smiling at Mr. Murphy and meet Alfrid. Danny beckoned wildly, and Alfrid slowly walked forward to join them.

Danny opened his mouth to speak, but Mr. Murphy beat him to it. "Mrs. Kelly," he said with a slight bow, "may I present to you Mr. Alfrid Swenson."

"How do you do, Mrs. Kelly?" Alfrid said, so quietly he could barely be heard.

"Very well, Mr. Swenson. Thank you," Ma said firmly and held out her right hand, her left wrapped firmly around Peg's shoulders. Alfrid took it, and for just a moment both he and Ma silently studied each other's faces. Danny tried to read what they were thinking, but Alfrid seemed as solemn as ever, and Ma smiled, gently pulling her hand away.

"I thank you for taking such good care of Danny

and Peg. You and your wife ... You were both very kind."

Danny didn't like the way Ma was talking, as though this were all a part of the past. He edged close to Ma, his back to Mr. Murphy, and said, "Ma, you'll like the farm. It's near the river, and there's a woods and green hills. Maybe it's like Ireland. When you see it you'll know."

Ma bent to kiss his forehead. "Oh, Danny, the way you go on! It's so good to hear your voice again. I've missed you all so terribly much. I've been so lonely for you. I can't wait to see the others too—Mike and Frances and little Petey. Do you know that Megan has learned to read and write? She sent another letter only two weeks ago."

Peg burrowed into the skirt of Ma's long coat and clung tightly.

"I help Mr. Swenson," Danny continued. "He told me I'm as good as any farmhand. And Peg and I go to school. And—"

"And I've got a kitten named Whiskers!" Peg chimed in.

The station platform was empty except for their little family and Mr. Murphy. Danny shot Mr. Murphy a look of irritation, hoping he'd understand and go away.

Instead, Mr. Murphy said, "The air is cold, Mrs. Kelly. I suggest that we take you out of this chill."

"I'm sorry." Alfrid looked embarrassed. "I should have thought."

Danny scowled. Alfrid didn't need to apologize. Anyone could see that he was just being kind and patient. Why did Mr. Murphy have to poke his nose in where he wasn't wanted?

"I understand I'm to stay with a Mrs. Banks," Ma said, her left arm still pressing Peg tightly to her side. "I would like to meet this kind lady."

"Of course," Alfrid said, clumsily picking up Ma's satchel. "You must be tired from the trip. I'm sure you'd like to rest." For some reason Alfrid's face flushed a deep red.

Ma got a mischievous twinkle in her eyes. "I'm not the least bit tired, Mr. Swenson. I have a strong constitution. I believe that Danny described me to you as 'strong as a whole team of horses.'" She laughed, and Mr. Murphy laughed, too, but Alfrid looked even more solemn.

"The buggy is hitched by the big oak tree," Alfrid said. He reached for Ma's elbow, but Ma had Danny in one hand and Peg in the other and was already striding toward the buggy.

Danny couldn't believe that Mr. Murphy didn't have enough sense to leave. He actually walked with Alfrid to the buggy and looked up at Ma. "Since you'll be visiting in town for a while with Katherine Banks, I'll be sure to be seeing you now and then," he said. He tipped his hat, adding, "A pleasant good day to one and all."

Alfrid climbed into the buggy and flicked the reins. "Katherine's house is high on the hill with a good view of the river," he said. "She asked me to take your things there and then—if you were agreeable—to bring you to the store to meet her."

"Most of the time I have a pleasant nature and do try hard to be agreeable," Ma teased.

Alfrid's face flushed again. "I didn't mean ... Perhaps I chose the wrong words."

Ma laughed again. "I know what you meant, Mr. Swenson. I was trying to ease the strain with a little humor."

Alfrid looked at Ma in bewilderment. "I don't understand."

"To make our meeting less difficult for both of us," Ma said.

Alfrid nodded. "I see."

"You're a kind man, Mr. Swenson," Ma said. "I am grateful to you for your loan to help pay for my train fare to St. Joseph. The family that employed me gave me a parting gift of a coat, which had belonged to one of their daughters, my satchel, and some money. I'll turn the full amount over to you. It is almost enough to pay you back."

"But I—I do not expect the money to be repaid," Alfrid stammered.

"Nevertheless, it will be repaid. I greatly appreciate your kindness, but I'm an independent woman, and I'll not feel right owing you a single cent." Ma beamed and hugged Peg and Danny to her again. "Now tell me, Mr. Swenson, have these two rapscallions given you a great deal of trouble?"

Alfrid's eyebrows shot up. "Oh, no!" he insisted. "They've been very good children."

Peg giggled, and Alfrid looked confused. "I see. It was another joke." He turned his attention to the horses. The road curved upward, and the pace of the buggy slowed as the team strained against the slope. Through the trees Danny caught glimpses of the Missouri River, silver in the thin sunlight.

"There's much we need to learn about each other, Mr. Swenson," Ma said gently.

"I'll drive you out to the farm after you've met Mrs. Banks," Alfrid said. "I'll show you around the property and give you a list of my assets. The farm has provided a steady income, although there is little actual cash because most of the profit has been invested in more cattle, more land, and larger crops."

Ma reached over and rested her gloved fingertips on his arm. "You are a kind man, and generous to want to share all this with me. But it is *you* I want to learn about, not your property. Do you like to read books? To tell stories? Do you like to dance?"

Alfrid looked at Ma warily, as though suspecting another joke. "There have been dances at the church," he said seriously, "but I never learned to dance. There was never time."

"How well I know," Ma said. "As a girl I loved to dance, but there was always so much work to be done. It's been a long, long time since I've had the chance to go to a dance." She grinned. "At the place where I worked, the houseman played the fiddle. Sometimes, when the master and mistress were away, the rest of us would gather in the kitchen, and he'd play a jig that could set boots to dancing on their own. The cook and I would pick up our skirts and away we'd go through the old steps, with the others laughing and clapping. Oh, it was grand fun!"

Danny laughed as he pictured it. It didn't hurt so much to imagine that part of Ma's life, now that she was here in St. Joseph.

Alfrid pulled the horses to a stop in front of a white clapboard house. He jumped down and hitched them to the post at the side of the road, then held up a hand to help Ma from the buggy.

As Ma stepped to the ground, she closed her eyes and took a deep breath. "The air here is clean, as it was in Ireland. Not quite the same, but close to it, and not a bit like New York."

She led the way to Katherine's front door. "Katherine said to tell you that your room will be the second bedroom on the right," Alfrid said.

Ma took the satchel from his hands. "I'll wash my face and hands," she said, "and be with you soon."

"I want to go with you!" Peg said, and ran after her mother.

Danny followed Alfrid back to the buggy and sat beside him on the front seat. Alfrid didn't speak. Danny couldn't stand it, and finally he blurted out, "Well? Wasn't I right about Ma?"

"She's an exceptionally beautiful woman," Alfrid said.

Danny shrugged. "I guess," he said, "but I wasn't thinking about that. I meant the rest of it."

Alfrid leaned back and patted Danny's shoulder. "I'm sure she's everything you said she was. Even more. Your mother's a very—um—powerful woman."

Powerful? Was that good or bad? Just what did Alfrid mean? Danny sneaked a look at Alfrid, but it was impossible to read his face.

11

AT THE FARM Peg wouldn't leave her mother's side, even though Danny pulled her away, whispering into her ear, "Leave Ma and Alfrid be."

"No!" Peg said stubbornly. "I want to stay with Ma."

"Then at least keep quiet and let Ma and Alfrid talk to each other," Danny insisted.

Peg simply jerked out of his grasp and ran to hang onto Ma's hand.

Danny went back to the house. As he walked into the kitchen, Melba was saying to Gussie, "She's pleasant enough, I guess, but hardly the type I'd expect Alfrid to like."

"Why shouldn't he like her?" Gussie asked. "I do. She's as friendly as down home, and a beauty."

Melba carried a tray into the dining room. "I'd hardly say that. She's a little thin for most men's tastes, I would think."

Gussie suddenly spotted Danny. "Well, Danny," she said, "I like your Ma."

"Thanks," Danny answered.

Melba returned to the kitchen, her cheeks pink with embarrassment, the empty tray at her side. She didn't acknowledge Danny as she began loading the tray again with platters of sliced bread and meats. "Gussie, we need another place at the table," Melba said. "You've set it one short."

Gussie counted on her fingers, then shook her head. "There's a place for everybody."

"I've asked Ennie Pratka to join us for dinner," Gussie said.

"Mrs. Pratka!" Danny blurted out. "Why?"

"She's a near neighbor and a good friend," Melba said. "Your mother will want to meet the neighbors, won't she?"

"Uh, I guess," Danny muttered, not knowing what else to say. He wandered into the parlor and kicked at the footstool. Mrs. Pratka would probably be her usual bossy self, and Danny didn't want anything to hurt Ma's good impression of Alfrid and his home. Aunt Melba, with her sighs and resigned looks, was bad enough.

Ma came in glowing, her cheeks pink and her eyes sparkling. A few strands of her hair had come loose, and she tried to tuck them back into the bun at her neck. "The land is beautiful, and there's even a cluster of young birch trees off to the south that could well be a faerie ring if it were in the right place."

"What's a faerie ring?" Gussie asked.

"It's a part of the Irish magic," Ma said.

"Ma tells the best stories," Peg said. "I like the scary ones—like about the pookas who change shape in the night and thunder down the dark roads."

Gussie leaned forward eagerly. "I love a good story!"

"Then you'll hear them all," Ma promised.

Alfrid had come in behind Ma, and Danny was aware that he was intently studying her. *He doesn't understand her*, Danny thought. *Was there something else I should have told him? Something I left out?*

The kitchen door suddenly burst open, and Ennie Pratka sailed into the room. In her hands was a large, fragrant mince pie. She stopped and stared at Ma. Danny was surprised to see that the look in Mrs. Pratka's eyes was exactly like the look in Wilmer's eyes when he and Danny had first met and he was sizing up Danny for a fistfight.

Melba stepped forward and hugged Mrs. Pratka with one arm, taking the pie from her with the other hand. "Dear, dear Ennie," she said. "Let me introduce you to the children's mother, Mrs. Kelly. Alfrid, don't just stand there. Help Ennie off with her wrap. Mrs. Kelly, Ennie has long been Alfrid's and Olga's dearest friend."

Ma was taller than Aunt Melba and Mrs. Pratka. She had to look down at them. She held out a hand to each. "Ennie, it's my great pleasure to meet such a good friend," she said. "And Melba, how kind you have been to Alfrid and to the children, too. Alfrid hasn't had to tell me all that you've done. I can see it."

"Oh. Well. My goodness," Melba murmured, suddenly flustered.

"I hope that you'll both be my friends, too," Ma said, "so please call me Noreen."

Gussie turned from the stove. "Dinner's ready whenever you are," she said cheerfully.

"Gussie," Melba mumbled, her lips thin with irritation. "It's my place to invite our guests to dinner, not yours! What will Mrs. Kelly think?"

Noreen laughed and winked at Gussie. "I'm thinking that it all smells so grand I can't wait to eat it."

Danny trailed at the rear as they filed into the dining room. Gussie stopped him by grasping his shoulder.

"Watch out for Mrs. Pratka," she said. "She hasn't given up yet."

It didn't take Danny long to realize that Gussie was right. Mrs. Pratka immediately steered the conversation to cooking, and Ma admitted that she probably couldn't hold a candle to Ennie as a cook.

"The cook where I worked taught me how to make many dishes," Ma said, "but when I lived with my family, we often didn't have much to eat. We relied mostly on potatoes and cabbage, which were filling."

Melba raised her eyebrows, and Mrs. Pratka looked smugly satisfied.

Conversation during the rest of the meal went just as badly. Alfrid didn't speak but toyed miserably with his food. Mrs. Pratka continually alluded to Ma's lack of experience in running a prosperous farm, compared to her own abundant skills. Danny winced when once again she quoted the late Tyrus Pratka's remark that she should win a gold medal for her cooking.

Ma kept her peace, simply agreeing with everything, until Mrs. Pratka glanced at Danny and Peg and said, "You have such lovely children. How could you bear to give them away?"

Ma put down her fork and leaned across the table toward Mrs. Pratka. Her eyes glittered with tears and anger. "I couldn't bear to. It was the most painful thing I have ever had to do in my entire life, more painful even than losing the husband I loved with all my heart. Each day we were apart I missed my children more than the day before.

"I have many faults, Mrs. Pratka," Ma added, "and one is that I am a proud woman. Yet I would choose any humiliation, any hurt, in order to be with my children again." She straightened, sitting tall, shoulders back and chin held high, and her words were spaced with determination. "We will never speak of this again. I know you understand me."

But Mrs. Pratka refused to bend. "I think we understand each other, Mrs. Kelly."

After a few minutes Gussie carried the dishes from the table and brought in Mrs. Pratka's mince pie, which she had cut into generous pieces.

"I'll serve," Mrs. Pratka said proudly, and reached for the pie, the serving wedge, and the plates, while Gussie handed forks around.

"Guests first, family last," Mrs. Pratka said pointedly as she dished a piece of the pie onto a plate. "For you, Mrs. Kelly."

Ma passed the piece on to Melba. "No, thank you. None for me," she said.

Ennie flushed. "I made it for you." She quickly glanced at Alfrid. "That is, for Alfrid and for you, too. At least try a small piece." The thin smile she gave Ma made Danny shiver. "You could use a little meat on your bones."

Ma smiled back. "You seem to have more than enough to spare." She paused. "I'm speaking of the pie, of course." She accepted the small wedge of pie Mrs. Pratka cut for her, took only a tiny taste, then turned to Alfrid with a series of questions about the town of St. Joseph.

Danny was relieved when dinner was over but horrified when Ma said, "I had better get busy and pack the children's things."

"Ma!" Danny cried. "We live *here* now!"

"I'll be staying with Mrs. Banks for a while," Ma said. "I just thought that you and Peg would want to be with me."

"*I* do!" Peg piped up.

"You're taking the children?" Alfrid looked astounded. "But they're used to being here, and they have school to go to."

Danny stood close to Alfrid. "I can't go with you, Ma.

My—my father needs me." As Ma's eyes widened with surprise, he quickly added, "And the wedding will be soon, won't it? Then you'll come here to live."

Danny wondered if the others had seen Ma flinch. When she spoke, her voice was so strong he decided he must have imagined it. "It wouldn't be right not to give Alfrid the opportunity to get to know me," Ma said. "His offer of marriage was a kind one, but he should go into marriage sure that this is what he really wants." Quietly she added, "What we *both* really want."

"Come on, Ma!" Peg said, tugging at Ma's hand. "I'll show you my room, and we can pack my things."

Danny took a deep breath and looked at his mother squarely, hoping that she'd understand. "Take Peg if you want," he said, "but I'd like to stay here."

Ma's smile was loving as she tousled his hair. "I understand, Danny. I love you very much, and I'm proud of you."

As Ma ran up the stairs with Peg, Melba sucked in her breath, then let it out with a hiss. "Well, I never!" she said. "I do believe that Mrs. Kelly actually wants to be courted!"

"That's not what she said, Aunt Melba!" Danny protested.

Alfrid nodded as though Melba had spoken wisely. "Thank you for your advice, Melba," he said. "If that's what is on Noreen's mind, then I'll know how to proceed."

Melba let out a little gasp. Mrs. Pratka clutched her elbow and propelled her out of the room, saying loudly, "Let's see if we can lend a hand to Gussie." But Danny heard her add in a whisper, "We need to talk."

When they drove Ma and Peg to Katherine's house, not only Katherine was waiting for them; John Murphy was, too.

"This is a rare coincidence," he said as he jumped to

his feet and smiled broadly at Ma. "I had just stopped by for a few minutes to discuss with Mrs. Banks a change of feed for her horse."

Danny saw that Mr. Murphy had scrubbed so hard his skin was still red, and the high collar on his shirt was stiff with starch. Some coincidence! Danny scowled at him and said, "You're a blacksmith. What would you have to do with feeding Mrs. Banks's horse?"

"Danny! Don't be rude!" Ma warned.

But Mr. Murphy extended his smile to include Danny, too. "The lad was not being rude, just curious," he said. "To answer Danny's question, I am not just a blacksmith. I have a half interest in the livery stable as well." Mr. Murphy looked back to Ma. "Which could provide a very comfortable living for a small family."

Peg asked, "Do you help take care of the horses? Do you let your children ride them?"

"I have no children," he said, "never having been married."

Danny wished Mr. Murphy wouldn't keep staring at Ma. "Ma came to St. Joseph to get married to our father," he said.

Ma blushed. "*Foster* father," she said. "And you needn't explain, Danny. John heard the entire story while we rode together on the train."

John! Danny had felt warm and comfortable when he had heard Ma call Alfrid by his given name, but he didn't want her to be friendly to Mr. Murphy, too.

"I have a cat named Whiskers," Peg said to Mr. Murphy. "I wanted to bring him, but he hid and wouldn't come."

"You'll see him soon, Peg, when you and Ma—" Danny began.

"Here, Peg, let's take off your coat," Ma interrupted.

Katherine waved a hand toward the overstuffed chairs and sofa. "Everyone, please sit down," she said. "Who would like a cup of coffee or hot apple cider?" She grinned at Peg. "And who'd like to help eat the pan of shortbread I made?"

"Could I have a piece now?" Peg asked.

"Surely. Come and help me put some on a plate— some currant cakes, too. We'll let you pass them around."

As Katherine and Peg left the room, Ma removed her hat and coat. Before Danny knew what had happened, Mr. Murphy had steered her to a place next to him on the sofa. Alfrid sat down on a chair across from them.

Something was going wrong with his plan, and Danny didn't like it at all.

12

"PEG'S WITH HER mother, and you won't be needing me," Melba said to Alfrid when he and Danny returned to the farm that evening. "I'm wanted at home, so I'll be on my way tomorrow."

"I thought you'd stay for the wedding," Alfrid said.

Melba avoided his eyes and said only, "I've been away from home too long."

"It was good of you to help us," Alfrid said. "I can't thank you enough."

For some reason Danny didn't understand, Melba looked guilty instead of pleased. She smoothed down her skirts and spoke quickly. "I know Gussie's not much of a cook, but she'll do until your new wife takes over. In the meantime, if there's anything you want, just call on Ennie." Melba gave a long sigh. "Dear Ennie is so good-hearted, she's already offered to send over some baked goods now and then, and perhaps a roast and a few other things for your dinners."

"She needn't go to all that trouble," Alfrid said. "In fact, I wish she wouldn't." Now *he* looked guilty.

"Nonsense," Melba said. "Ennie truly cares for your welfare, Alfrid. I'm surprised you haven't seen that."

Danny couldn't stand it any longer. He rushed out to the kitchen, where Gussie was preparing to leave. "Ma is supposed to marry my fa—foster father," he blurted out, "but everybody tries to get in the way! I don't know what to do."

Gussie buttoned the last button on her coat and tied a scarf over her hair. "It's up to your Ma and to Mr. Swenson, not to you."

"But having them get married was my idea!"

Gussie nodded. "That's why your ma came out here, so why worry about it?" She opened the back door but turned before she stepped outside. "Just stop your frettin' about whether they'll get married or not. There ain't nothin' you can do about it."

Danny just stared at the door after Gussie had closed it behind her. Oh, yes, there was something he could do. He just had to figure out what it was!

Alfrid rode into town to see Ma the next few evenings, but he came home as solemn and serious as when he left. Danny wished he would talk about Ma, but he didn't.

Gussie reported that just about every day while Danny was at school, Mrs. Pratka brought favorite dishes over to add to the noon meal and stayed to eat and chat with Alfrid.

"About what?" Danny demanded.

Gussie shrugged. "About nothin' very important. She does most of the talkin', but the mister's gettin' kind of used to her, I think, because now and then he has somethin' chatty to say hisself."

Danny groaned. He hurried outside to help Alfrid,

who was shoveling a path through the snow from the house to the barn. "Do you ever see Mr. Murphy, the blacksmith, when you're in town?" Danny asked him.

Alfrid nodded. "As a matter of fact, I do. He often stops at Mrs. Banks's home for a short visit."

"To see Mrs. Banks?" Danny managed to ask.

"To see your mother," Alfrid said. He handed Danny the shovel. "There isn't much more to do here. Could you finish this job?" Before Danny could ask him another question, Alfrid went into the barn.

Miss Clark kept Danny after school one afternoon. "Danny, you don't have your mind on your work," she said. "I had to call on you twice to recite before you even heard me, then we both discovered you weren't prepared."

"I'm sorry," Danny mumbled. "I've had a lot to think about lately."

Miss Clark leaned her elbows on the desk and rested her chin in her hands. "Yes, you have, Danny. A lot of difficult things have happened to you, but you've handled them well. You usually seem to be able to think ahead, to plan for tomorrow. I admire that quality in you."

"A plan! That's what I need—a plan!" Danny said aloud.

Miss Clark looked puzzled. "A plan for what?" she asked.

Danny backed toward the door. "It's just something I have to work out for myself," he said.

Miss Clark shrugged. "All right, Danny. But don't forget what I said about keeping your mind on your schoolwork."

"I won't," he answered, and ran out the door and halfway home before he was out of breath.

During the rest of the walk he thought hard about both Mrs. Pratka and Mr. Murphy, trying to remember everything they had done and said, and an idea began to tickle the back of his mind. Danny laughed aloud as he suddenly knew what to do. Oh, he had a plan, all right. And it would begin with Mr. Murphy!

Danny didn't waste any time. As soon as he arrived at the farm he went straight to Alfrid and said, "I miss Ma and Peg, and I'd like to see them tonight. Will you take me with you when you go to visit them?"

Alfrid hesitated. "It will be a short visit. Tonight is another meeting, and it's important that I attend. Ralph Waldo Emerson will be the guest speaker."

"I'll go to the meeting with you, too," Danny said quickly. "You promised that when Mr. Emerson came to speak you'd take me to hear him." He had no wish to spend any more time than necessary with Mr. Murphy.

"I know I had promised," Alfrid said, "but tempers are high and I'm not sure it will be safe for you. The meeting hall is in a rough area, and ever since Kansas was granted statehood there have been more rabble-rousers than usual hanging about the streets. Lately they've been congregating on the street next to our meeting place, and they try to interrupt the speakers. Maybe it would be better if you stayed with your mother and I picked you up when the meeting is over."

"I'd really like to hear Mr. Emerson speak. Miss Clark read us a poem Mr. Emerson wrote. I'm not afraid," Danny insisted. "I'll be with you."

Alfrid nodded as he thought. "If there's any sign of trouble, I suppose we can leave quickly."

"Then can I go?"

"Yes," Alfrid finally agreed. "You may go. Just be sure you finish all your schoolwork."

"I will!" Danny ran into the house, shouted a hello in Gussie's direction, and dashed into the dining room, flinging off his coat, hat, and scarf as he ran. He rummaged in the drawer of the sideboard until he found paper and ink, then seated himself at the table to write.

"Things To Be Bought in Town," he headed the paper. Under this he made a list:

Soda for Alfrid's indigestion, due to being made to eat too much heavy food.

Stuff to make a poultice for boils, which come on from trying to digest too much heavy food.

Headache powders for Alfrid, who gets terrible headaches every afternoon after being stuffed with all that heavy food at his noon dinner.

Just to make the list look more official, he added "flour" and "salt." He folded the paper in thirds, wrote on the back, "Private. Do not read this," and took it to the kitchen, where Mrs. Pratka would be sure to see it. He knew her curiosity would get the best of her, and she'd read it. She was so sensitive about her cooking, this letter was bound to chase her away.

"Whatcha got there?" Gussie asked him.

"A shopping list," Danny said. He started to read. "Soda, flour, salt."

"I think we got plenty of salt," Gussie said. "You could cross that out." She thought a moment. "How come you're puttin' together a shoppin' list?"

"I want to be helpful," Danny said. He held out the paper so she could see the back. "Do you want to read it?"

"Private?" Gussie snickered and rolled her eyes. "No, thanks. I'm not much for readin', and a *private* shoppin' list about flour and soda ain't that interestin'."

Satisfied, Danny laid the list on a shelf where it could easily be seen. "Leave it right here, then. Promise?"

"Promise," Gussie said. "Here—take these plates and

put them on the table when you go back to the dining room."

Danny charged through his arithmetic problems and spelling words and wolfed down his supper. He was so impatient he could hardly stand it until he and Alfrid were in the buggy and off to St. Joseph.

"What has Ma been doing while she's staying with Mrs. Banks?" Danny asked. "No one's told me."

Alfrid's mouth turned down, and his words were almost bitter. "She's been cleaning Mrs. Banks' house and the house of the woman next door to earn money. She insists that what I sent her for train fare was merely a loan, and she's intent on returning to me every penny."

"Ma's like that," Danny said. "She wouldn't want you to think she had no pride."

Alfrid's brow wrinkled. "Is that why she's paying me back?"

"I'm sure of it," Danny said. "If you knew Ma—"

Alfrid interrupted, his voice so low he seemed to be talking to himself. "I don't know her. I really don't know her at all."

"Maybe I could tell you more about her," Danny offered, although he didn't know how or where to begin.

But Alfrid shook his head. "Not just now. Let me tell you what to expect at the meeting we'll be going to tonight. A few days ago the Southern states seceded from the Union and organized a Confederacy with Jefferson Davis as their president. The talk now is that Missouri will go with them...."

His interest caught, Danny listened intently, forgetting about Ma until he and Alfrid arrived at Katherine Banks's home.

Ma met Danny at the door with a vigorous hug that lifted him off his feet. "I've missed you!" she cried. "How's my darlin' boy?"

Danny held his mother tightly, wishing with all his

heart that she'd set a date for the wedding. Then he could enjoy having Ma and Alfrid together and forget all about Mrs. Pratka and Mr. Murphy.

Peg ran to hug Danny, and as he swung her around, he heard Ma say politely, "Good evening, Alfrid."

Alfrid answered every bit as quietly and formally, "Good evening, Noreen."

That didn't sound like Ma. It didn't sound like Alfrid, either. What was the matter with them?

Danny and Alfrid were no sooner seated in the parlor than a loud knock came at the door. Ma rushed to answer it, and Alfrid stared down at his hands. Danny knew who the visitor was going to be. That was fine with him. There was no time like the present to put his plan into action.

Ma's footsteps were light as she reentered the parlor, and her face was bright with smiles. "Look who's here," she announced. "John Murphy."

"Ah, and there's that fine lad, Danny," Mr. Murphy said. He shook hands with Alfrid first, then Danny, and bent to kiss Peg, who—to Danny's dismay—flung her arms around his neck in a hug.

"Here's a little something for you, Noreen," Mr. Murphy said, and pulled from his pocket a twist of peppermints, handing it to Ma with a flourish. So! Mr. Murphy was bringing Ma little gifts, was he? Danny could easily think of something for Alfrid to bring to Ma. Maybe a flower? But with the snow there were no flowers blooming. Oh well, he'd figure that out later. Now it was time to carry out his plan.

Peg came to sit on Alfrid's lap, resting her head against his shoulder. "How is my Whiskers?" she asked. "Does he miss me?"

"He looks for you at times," Alfrid said. "And he sleeps in your room, as he has always done."

"Is my bed still in the same place?" she asked. "And my doll bed?"

"Yes," Alfrid said. "Right where you left them."

Katherine arrived home, Andrew MacNair with her, and everyone jumped up to greet the new arrivals. Katherine's cheeks were glowing, and her eyes sparkled. "It's such a cold night," she said as she pulled off her gloves and rubbed her hands together briskly. "Let's warm up with some hot spiced cider."

Danny was pleased. Having so many people around would make his job easier. He waited until everyone in the room was busy chattering and passing around the mugs of cider, then tugged at Mr. Murphy's sleeve, pulling him aside from the rest.

"I haven't had much chance to talk with you," Danny said.

Mr. Murphy looked pleased. "I'd enjoy a bit of conversation with you, Danny. Did you have anything in particular in mind?"

"No," Danny said, making sure none of the others could hear him. "I was just thinking how it is a good thing Mr. Swenson's house has so many rooms, since Ma has so many children."

Mr. Murphy's eyebrows rose, and Danny hurried to continue. "I remember that you said something about your income providing a comfortable living for a small family. Well, we Kellys couldn't be called a small family."

"But your brothers and sisters have new homes now, and—"

Danny didn't let Mr. Murphy finish his sentence. "Do you think Ma will rest until we're all together again? No indeed. Oh, the fine times we've had, singing and yelling and squabbling until the wee hours of the morning. We're a noisy lot, there's no denying it."

Mr. Murphy frowned. "That's not the way Noreen has described her children."

Danny leaned close to whisper, "Of course not. If your children were so wild that they tore up the furniture and scared off the neighbors, what would you say?"

"Danny." Alfrid's voice so close behind him made Danny jump. "It's time to go."

"I'm going to the meeting, too," Andrew said. "I'll ride with you."

As the three of them put on their coats and said their good-byes, Danny didn't dare to meet Mr. Murphy's eye. He felt pleased with himself. He'd given the man something to chew on, all right. Mr. Murphy would want little to do with Ma after what Danny had told him tonight.

Seated between the two men he admired most, Alfrid and Andrew, Danny was spellbound both by the distinct, ringing tones of Mr. Emerson's voice and by the urgency of his antislavery message. Tears came to Danny's eyes as Mr. Emerson described the dreadful treatment of slaves in the Southern states. Even the noise from the street outside didn't distract him.

After the talk Danny went with Alfrid to the podium to shake Mr. Emerson's hand.

"I'll help, too!" he promised.

Mr. Emerson looked at Danny with great seriousness. "Thank you, young man," he said, and Danny was elated.

He followed Alfrid from the building, and his exalted mood shattered as they were confronted by a jostling, jeering group of men who yelled insults at the abolitionists. The protesters' shadows jumped grotesquely under the flickering gaslight, distorted by the thin, damp mists from the river which carried the sour, oily smell of bilge water from ships at anchor.

"Ignore those men," Alfrid said. He gripped Danny's hand and strode toward the stables, where he'd left the horses and buggy.

They had gone only a few yards when someone called

to Alfrid. It was one of the meeting's organizers, the short, heavyset man Danny remembered as having urged Alfrid's support. Alfrid halted, and for a few moments the two men were intent on their conversation. Danny walked on slowly, looking down the street. A few yards away, a man stood in the shadow of the building, staring back at him.

Danny sucked in his breath and squinted, trying to see more clearly. Wasn't the man Dr. Mundy? He was. He had to be. Suddenly gripped by a fear that made cold drops of sweat break out along his backbone, Danny realized that if he had seen Dr. Mundy, then Mundy had seen him.

13

THREE MEN ANGRILY elbowed past Danny, blocking his view of the man in the shadows. By the time they had passed, the man had disappeared.

Danny's heart was still pounding. He tried to calm himself. He wasn't sure the man was Dr. Mundy. In fact, he probably wasn't. Dr. Mundy would have come after Danny. But the man had been watching him. Never mind. He was gone now, and there was no point in chasing after bad luck.

Danny turned to rejoin Alfrid, but Alfrid had disappeared, too. He pushed through the crowd on the street, toward the spot where Alfrid had been standing. "Alfrid?" Danny called. "Father?"

"Danny!" a muffled voice called back. Danny spun around and noticed a division about four feet wide between two buildings. It was dark in the passageway and hard to see.

"I'm coming," Danny shouted, and stepped into the

darkness. He felt his way along the passage, using one of the brick walls as a guide. Twice he stumbled over debris, and once, while he was on all fours, something ran over his gloved hands. He scrambled up, shuddering. A rat!

"Alfrid!" he called again, but this time there was no answer. Frightened, Danny careened through the darkness toward the patch of lighter sky. Just a few feet more and he'd be there.

He stumbled noisily into the open space, finally managing to catch his balance. "Alfrid?" he whispered. There was no response.

Danny glanced to each side. Piles of crates towered nearby, their shadows creating blocks of darkness too deep to penetrate. The clamor in the street seemed far away, and the silence in this alley was as oppressive as a smothering quilt. The air crackled with danger, making the hair rise on the back of Danny's neck and along his arms. He'd never been so terrified in his life.

He had to get back to the street. Slowly, his legs trembling, he began to back toward the passageway. But a shape suddenly flung itself from the shadows, looming up in front of him, and a hand clutched his shoulder in a painful grip.

"Danny Kelly, is it?" a sharp voice hissed, and a face thrust itself close to his own. "You know me. I told you I'd be back."

Mundy! Danny tried to pull away, but Mundy's fingers dug into his shoulder so deeply that he cried out.

"You shouldn't have run off like that." Mundy chuckled. "You're likely to lose your way in the dark and end up drowned in the river."

"Let go of me!" Danny said. "Alfrid—Mr. Swenson— will come to find me. He won't let you hurt me."

"Swenson, is that his name? The one who rode me out?"

"Don't you dare do anything to hurt Alfrid!"

Mundy chuckled evilly. "And who's going to stop me? It looks to me like you're in no position to help anyone, including yourself." He gave Danny a shake. Danny struggled with all his strength, but he was no match for Mundy.

"What do you want?" Danny cried.

Dr. Mundy laughed. "You and that Swenson fellow did me a favor," he said. "My fortunes have improved considerable since I saw you last. I sold my wagon and medicines to some poor fool and made the acquaintance of some Southern sympathizers here in Missouri. They're eager to dip into their pockets to support arms and an army, so I have been doing some fund-raising for the cause."

"I know what you're doing! You're stealing their money!" Danny wrestled against Mundy's grip. "You wouldn't help anybody! You're only collecting it for yourself!"

Mundy bent to whisper into Danny's face, his foul breath hot against Danny's cheek. The pain in Danny's arm and shoulder was now so intense that white lights flickered in front of his eyes, and his legs could scarcely hold him up. "How right you are, boy," Mundy said. "I'm doing well for myself now, better than I ever have before." He snickered. "Some might say I should thank you for your meddling, but I have an old score to settle with you. Poor little orphan boy. Tomorrow they'll find your body floating in the river."

"Let me go!" Danny shouted. He thrashed and kicked wildly, but Mundy's hold remained firm. With all his might Danny tried to jerk away, but suddenly a large, dusty burlap sack was thrown over his head, nearly strangling him, and whipped down to enfold his body. Choking and coughing, he felt his arms being strapped to his sides as a rope was wound around him.

Then he felt himself jerked off his feet and jolted roughly from side to side. Mundy had picked him up and was carrying him—where? To the river?

Alfrid! Ma! Danny thought, realizing he'd never see them again. Desperate, terrified, Danny kicked and struggled with all his might, trying to get free.

"Stop that!" Mundy snapped. Danny felt Mundy stumble, and his shoulder slammed against something hard.

Danny cried out in pain, and he squirmed and fought all the harder. He thrust out a foot and heard a crash.

"Danny? Where are you?"

It was Alfrid's voice, and he was nearby.

Danny tried to yell but sucked in the dust from the burlap. Only a strangled, choking sound came out.

"Danny!"

All at once Danny went flying. He landed on his back, momentarily stunned. The force of his fall had loosened the rope, and he managed to claw his way from the bag.

Staggering to his feet, still coughing, Danny took a deep breath, trying to clear his head and lungs. Before him, two dark figures grappled on the ground. One suddenly rose to a sitting position, raising his right arm high. Moonlight glinted on the blade of Mundy's knife.

Danny lunged at Mundy and used the only weapon he had. He sank his teeth into Mundy's right wrist, tasting blood, and heard the knife clatter to the ground.

Howling with pain, Mundy gave Danny a blow that sent him reeling back, then scrambled into the darkest shadows. Danny regained his balance and took a few steps after Mundy, but Alfrid climbed unsteadily to his feet and shouted, "No! Danny! Stay with me!"

"*I'll get you!*" Mundy yelled at them, and they could hear his footsteps echoing down the alley.

"Let's catch him!" Danny gasped, then broke into a coughing fit that bent him double.

"He's a rat, running to his hole in the darkness," Alfrid said. "We'd never find him."

Danny shuddered, remembering the rat that had run over his hand. "You saved my life," he said to Alfrid.

"And you saved mine."

Danny wrapped his arms around Alfrid and began to sob. "I'm sorry, Alfrid! I'm sorry. He almost killed you, and it was all my fault!"

Alfrid's tone was gentle. "You've said all that needs to be said. There's no point in dwelling on it."

"Oh, Father!" Danny said, burrowing his face into Alfrid's shoulder, "I love you!"

"And I love you," Alfrid said quietly. He held Danny securely until there were no more tears.

"Will Dr. Mundy come back again?" Danny whispered.

"Don't worry," Alfrid said. "Remember, he's just like a rat. If we cornered him, he'd turn and fight, but we frightened him away, and I think he'll stay away. He had his try at revenge. That should satisfy him."

Danny wasn't so sure. Mundy wasn't likely to leave the area—not while his scheme to steal money was succeeding. Danny wanted to tell Alfrid what Mundy had said, but he knew that Alfrid would tell the marshal, and if Mundy wasn't captured right away, he might try to harm Alfrid. Danny couldn't let that happen, so he kept the information to himself.

"We've lingered here long enough," Alfrid said, and took Danny by the hand. "Let's go home."

The next day, after returning from school, still sore from Mundy's rough handling, Danny headed for the kitchen. The list he had written was still there, but not where he had left it. He shoved it into his pocket and asked Gussie, "Did Mrs. Pratka read this?"

"She asked what it was, and I said it was only a shoppin' list. I saw her pick it up, but don't fuss about it. If what you writ was all so private, you shouldn't have left it out for anyone to come across."

"Did Mrs. Pratka stay for dinner?"

Gussie cocked her head, rubbing one finger on her chin. "No, she didn't. Seemed like something was stuck in her craw. She brought a pie with her and some stuff in a parcel. She poked around the kitchen for a few minutes, then picked up her parcel and went home. At least she left the pie."

Danny turned his back on Gussie so she wouldn't see his grin as she continued. "When I seen that the widow Pratka wasn't gonna stay, I boiled up a chicken for the mister's noon meal. It turned out kinda tough so there's plenty left over to slice cold for supper, and there's most of the pie."

For just an instant Danny's stomach rumbled with hunger, and he wondered if he'd done the right thing. He did enjoy the leftovers from the noon meals Mrs. Pratka had made. With Gussie doing the cooking, it would be a different matter. Oh, well, Ma would soon be here and set everything to rights.

That evening Danny asked Alfrid if he could go along to see Ma again. He had to know if his plan had worked with Mr. Murphy, too.

Ma seemed quieter than usual. Occasionally she glanced toward the front door, but Mr. Murphy didn't show up. Danny wasn't sure whether his wishful thinking or Katherine's managing was responsible, but he, Peg, and Katherine ended up in the kitchen, leaving Ma and Alfrid alone in the parlor to chat. Danny couldn't have been happier. With Mr. Murphy out of the way, Ma and Alfrid would have a chance to discover they were both grand people, and Ma would set a wedding date.

As Alfrid and Danny were preparing to leave, Danny managed to whisper to Alfrid, "When will Ma come out to the farm again?"

Alfrid looked intently at Ma for a moment, then he turned back to Danny. "Why not invite your mother and

Peg and Katherine now?" he suggested. "Maybe they'd agree to come for dinner Sunday."

Danny was so excited it was hard to stand still as he relayed the invitation. He looked to his mother hopefully, but it was Katherine who spoke first.

"I'm sure we'd all love to come."

"Yes," Ma added quickly. "Would you like us to bring the food?" She paused, her eyes now on Alfrid. "Or will Mrs.—will one of your neighbors help with the cooking?"

"No!" Danny said. "Mrs. Pratka won't be there. Gussie and I will do all the cooking!"

"Me, too!" Peg volunteered. "I want to help, too!"

Happier than he'd been since the excitement of Ma's arrival, Danny agreed.

On the way home he wished Alfrid would talk about Ma and about the fine conversation they'd had, but Alfrid was silent, immersed in his own thoughts. Danny let his own mind drift ahead to Sunday. He was glad that Ma wanted to come. It was time she began to feel at home on the farm—their farm.

Gussie refused to work on Sunday. "It's my day off," she said. " 'Sides, I got me a beau, and he's comin' over to meet my ma and pa." Her expression grew serious. "He's goin' down to Atlanta to sign on with the Confederate Army."

"We're not at war!" Danny said.

"We will be soon. Everybody's sayin' so." Gussie paused. "I may not see him for a long time, so I don't want to be here cookin' dinner. You understand, don't you?"

Danny shrugged. "I'll make the dinner myself."

"Wonder why the widow Pratka ain't been over," Gussie said. "Maybe if you give her a holler, she'll do the cookin'."

"No," Danny answered quickly. "You just tell me what to do, and I'll do it."

Gussie nodded. "I'll put together a milk pudding the day before, and you know how to clean the carrots and potatoes. Do you think you can roast a chicken?"

"If you show me how."

"Then there's nothin' to worry about," Gussie stated. "It's goin' to be a fine party."

A fine party? With no one to help him cook? Danny almost wished Ma wasn't coming.

No sooner had their guests arrived on Sunday afternoon than it began to snow heavily. Katherine lifted the curtains to glance from the parlor window. "Maybe we should head back to town," she said.

"But you just got here!" Danny cried. "Anyhow, it's started snowing so heavily you wouldn't be able to find the way." He had worked hard on the preparations for dinner, and he wanted everything to go smoothly. They couldn't leave!

Katherine glanced at Ma, a worried look in her eyes. "I'm afraid he's right," she said.

Ma gave Danny a reassuring smile. "We won't think about the snowfall," she said. "There's a fine dinner cooking, and good company, and we'll have a grand afternoon."

Peg, with Whiskers firmly in one arm, tugged at her mother's skirts. "Ma, will you sing for us?"

"Oh, please do," Katherine said. "Danny told us you have a beautiful voice, but I haven't heard you sing."

Ma blushed a little and laughed. "The Irish songs I know may seem strange to you."

"I would like very much to hear them," Alfrid said.

So Ma stood by the windows, the light from outside creating a gleaming ring around her hair, and sang of the green hills and valleys and of loves and families left behind.

Katherine's eyes were damp, and she was fumbling

for a handkerchief that she'd tucked into her sleeve, when Ma suddenly broke into a rollicking tune, ending it by lifting her skirts to her ankles, her feet flashing in a quick fancy dance step.

"Do it again, Ma! Again!" Peg clapped her hands.

But Danny jumped to his feet shouting, "Something's burning!"

He raced to the kitchen, Ma right behind him. Grabbing a cloth to protect his hands, he swung the kettle of potatoes out from the fireplace. The water had boiled away, and those on the bottom had scorched.

"We'll save the ones on top," Ma said as she scooped them into a bowl and covered them with another cloth to keep them warm. "Shall we see about the rest of the meal?"

Danny opened the door of the brick oven. "I think the chicken is done," he said. He poked at a drumstick with a long-handled fork, and the drumstick fell off into the bottom of the pan.

"I like it well done," Ma said. "What else will we be having?"

"Carrots," Danny said with a sinking feeling. The carrots were still sitting in a pan of water on the table. He'd forgotten to put them on the fire.

Ma gave him a quick hug. "They're as good raw as they are cooked," she said. "Why don't you pour off the water and put them into a bowl, and we'll get the meal on the table?"

Peg, hovering in the doorway, made a face. "Something smells awful!" she said.

"Get out of here!" Danny growled at her.

"You said I could help."

"Maybe you could put the bread on the table," Ma told her. She turned to Danny. "Do you have a little jelly or maybe some preserves to go with it?"

"I'll carry this!" Before anyone could stop her, Peg

grabbed the heavy bowl that held the milk pudding, struggled to keep her grip on it, and dropped it. The bowl broke, and the pudding splashed and slithered across the floor.

Danny cried out, lunged toward Peg, and slid into the pudding. He sat down hard on the wooden floor.

"Careful, Danny. I'll help you up," Ma said. She held out a hand but missed her footing on the slippery floor and landed on top of Danny.

"Ma!" Peg rushed toward her mother, skidded, and fell flat. Peg raised her face, pudding dripping from her nose and chin, and Ma began to laugh.

Katherine and Alfrid rushed into the room. Alfrid tried to raise Ma up, but she was helpless with laughter. Finally she struggled to her feet. Katherine had pulled Peg and Danny up and began cleaning them off.

Alfrid looked at Ma with bewilderment and said, "I don't understand why you were laughing. You had a bad fall and could have been hurt."

Ma rubbed her right elbow. "I'll have a lump here all right," she said, "but there's nothing like a good laugh to take away the pain."

Katherine handed Ma a towel. "I've dried Peg's dress the best I could," she said. "But the back of your skirt is pretty well stained."

"It will wash," Ma said.

"Peg ruined the pudding!" Danny said, Although he'd had to laugh along with Ma, he was now beginning to get angry at Peg all over again.

But Ma's spirits weren't daunted. She scooped up Peg, who was puckering up to cry, and said, "Let's enjoy the rest of this good dinner Danny has made for us. I don't know about the rest of you, but I'm hungry."

"I am, too!" Katherine said.

Danny struggled to get his feelings under control. "Then sit down at the table, and I'll bring in the dinner. Just don't let Peg help anymore!"

He soon decided the others must be hungrier than he was. The chicken was so overdone Alfrid had to use a spoon along with the meat fork in order to lift portions to the plates. The potatoes tasted awful, even with the butter Danny slathered over them. Ma cheerfully crunched away on the raw carrots. Gussie's bread was doughy at the bottom, but everyone ate it without complaint.

After dinner, when the dishes were cleared, washed, and put away, and the last traces of the pudding cleaned off the floor, they all moved back to the parlor. Alfrid began lighting more lamps. "With the weather the way it is—" he began.

Ma suddenly put a hand on his arm. "Shhh! Listen," she said. She tilted her head and whispered, "I think it's stopped snowing."

Peg ran to the window and peered out into the dark. "The snow's not very deep," she reported. "But it's pretty. Come and look, Ma. The moon is shining on the snow and making it yellow and red."

"Yellow and red?" Danny asked. "Peg sometimes—" He stopped as he suddenly felt that something was seriously wrong.

Alfrid shoved back his chair and ran to the kitchen at the same time Danny did, throwing open the kitchen door. Here the red and gold light was blinding, a whoosh of sparks and flame.

The haystack nearest to the barn was on fire!

14

DANNY GRABBED A bucket. "Everybody! C'mon! We'll get water from the well!" he shouted, trying to squeeze past Alfrid. "Ma! Katherine! Help us!"

But Alfrid grabbed his arm and pulled him back. "Wait!" he cautioned. "Listen!"

With an air-sucking, crackling roar a second haystack exploded into flame.

Ma gasped. "What's happening?"

Before Alfrid could answer, three figures on horseback galloped from behind the far haystack. Like black demons silhouetted against the flames, they raced toward the house. Terrified, Danny could hear his own heart pounding in his ears.

"Hang the abolitionists!" one of them yelled, and fired a handgun into the air.

Alfrid slammed and bolted the door. The men on horseback yelled and fired into the air as they headed for the front of the house. Peg screamed, and Danny squeezed his eyes shut, clapping his hands over his ears.

Alfrid immediately took charge. He put out the lamp so that the kitchen was lit only with the glow of the fireplace. "Stay out of the kitchen," he ordered. "There could be stray bullets. Noreen, take Peg into the hallway and sit under the staircase. It's the safest place I can think of." As Ma hesitated, Alfrid barked, "Now!" Ma swept up Peg and ran.

"Katherine, do you know how to use a gun?" Alfrid asked as he strode through the dining room into the parlor, Danny and Katherine right behind him. Katherine quickly extinguished the oil lamps in both rooms.

"Yes," she answered.

In the dim light Alfrid opened a cabinet and pulled out two rifles, ball, powder, and cap. "I've used these only for hunting game to stock the larder." Danny could hear the sadness in Alfrid's voice as he added, "I hate to put them to any other use. We'll shoot only to defend ourselves, only if there's no other choice."

Katherine glanced toward Ma and Peg in the darkness under the stairway. "Do you think those men will try to kill us?" she whispered.

"No," Alfrid said. "I think they're merely trying to terrorize us. Once Mundy feels he has his revenge—"

Mundy! The name left Danny breathless and trembling. Katherine was asking, "Mundy? Who is he?"

The riders had circled the house, and now Danny heard them make another turn past the front. This time one of the parlor windows shattered. Katherine gasped, and Danny started. He could hear Peg crying and Ma trying to comfort her.

"There's no time to explain," Alfrid told Katherine. Crouching beside the broken window, he fumbled through the pieces of broken glass and held up a small rock. "I don't think they'll actually shoot at us," he said. "They're enjoying their game of terror."

Danny didn't agree. That night in the alley Alfrid had

said that Mundy wouldn't bother them if they left him alone, and he'd been wrong. Now Danny was afraid that Alfrid was wrong once again.

"Katherine, go to one of the back windows," Alfrid said.

"What should I do?" Danny asked.

"Just stay down and be ready," Alfrid said. "If we must shoot, we will need you to help us reload quickly."

With a whoosh of air and a loud crackle, the light outside suddenly grew brighter. "Another haystack," Alfrid muttered.

Maybe the haystacks were just the beginning, Danny thought. Maybe Mundy would set fire to the barn next, or to the house. Danny couldn't bear just to wait and see what Mundy and his chums had planned for them. He and Alfrid should have a plan of their own.

Silently Danny crept into the kitchen where he could get a better view of the barn and field. He cautiously peeked from the window just in time to see the horsemen approaching the house once again. As they thundered past, Danny leapt back, striking the wall so hard that an object fell off a shelf, hitting him on the head.

"Ouch!" he muttered. As he put up a hand to rub his head, there was a loud blast from a handgun, and the kitchen window shattered. It hadn't been a rock this time. It had been a bullet. Danny dropped to the floor, shivering in the cold blast of air. There was no doubt in Danny's mind that when Mundy was ready he would try to kill them.

As he scrambled away from the broken glass his fingers touched a familiar object—the rough ball of twine. So that's what had hit him on the head! He was about to return the twine to the shelf when an idea came to him. This ball of twine might be the answer to their problem.

Excited, Danny quickly pulled on his coat and steathily opened the kitchen door. For his plan to succeed, Mundy

127

and the men with him would have to race around the house at least one more time. Danny hoped that their horses wouldn't be hurt, but he had to take that chance.

Danny crept out and down the stairs. As fast as he could, his fingers stiff and aching with the cold, he tied one end of the twine to the supports under the back step, about a foot above the ground. He tugged at the knot, making sure it was secure, then ran with the ball of twine, paying it out, until he arrived at the barn. There he tied the twine around a post, pulling the line taut. The men were behind the house now, whooping and yelling and riding fast.

He had barely secured the knot when he heard the horses approaching at a gallop. He sucked in his breath, flattening himself against the open barn door. Hoofprints had muddied the ground, so the dark twine wouldn't be as obvious as it would have been against clean snow.

When the first horse fell it was like a horrible nightmare, a wild jumble of screaming and shouting. The other horses tripped and stumbled, and the men on their backs went flying. A gun bounced on the ground near Danny's feet, and he snatched it up.

As the fallen horse staggered to its feet, Danny gave a loud sigh of relief. One by one, the horses ran off, reins swinging free and stirrups flapping from their empty saddles. One of the men on the ground lay without moving, his chest heaving as he breathed. A second man grabbed his left leg, rolling back and forth and groaning. Danny turned to see a third man stealthily creeping on hands and knees toward him. It was Mundy.

Danny whirled and aimed the gun.

At the same time Alfrid burst from the house. "Mundy! Stop where you are!" Alfrid ordered and raised his rifle.

Mundy hesitated, crouching like an animal.

"I mean what I say. If you try to harm my son I'll shoot you." There was an anger in Alfrid's voice that Danny had never heard there.

Mundy dropped flat, rested his forehead on his arms, and muttered angrily under his breath.

The door slammed open as Ma and Katherine ran from the house. Without taking his eyes from Mundy, Alfrid gave a sharp nod toward the other two men on the ground. "Will you see to them, please?" he asked the women.

They worked quickly in spite of the cold. Katherine and Alfrid bound the three men and secured them inside the barn, while Ma, Danny, and Peg scattered the remains of the smoldering haystacks and doused them with buckets of water.

As Ma and Katherine went ahead into the house, Danny hung back, telling Alfrid that Mundy had been collecting money for a Southern army and then keeping it.

"You should have told me sooner," Alfrid said. "Mundy was stealing. He should have been stopped."

"I was afraid to tell you. You said that if we left Mundy alone, he'd stay away from us. I didn't want him to come back and hurt you."

Alfrid put his hands on Danny's shoulders and looked deeply into his eyes. "My own father gave me a saying to live by. Supposedly it was first said by a British statesman named Edmund Burke, who lived during the last century. I want you to listen carefully and always remember these words: 'The only thing necessary for the triumph of evil is for good men to do nothing.'"

Danny nodded, repeating the words in his mind. "I won't forget. Ever."

Alfrid put his arm around Danny's shoulders, and they began to walk toward the house. "Mundy won't fare well with his Southern sympathizers when they hear what he's been up to," he said.

While Alfrid tacked boards over the broken windows, Ma heated some water so they could all wash their sooty hands and faces. Danny, who was exhausted, splashed his face gladly.

"I'm proud of you," Alfrid said to Danny. "You chose a good plan of action."

Danny beamed. "We work well together, you and I."

"That we do," Alfrid said.

The expression on Ma's face, however, wasn't one of agreement. "That was a very dangerous thing to do, Danny," she said. She turned to Alfrid. "I think we need to talk."

Danny didn't want any part of that talk. He scurried into the parlor, where he added some wood to the fire in the fireplace and lay in front of it, soaking up the warmth. He could hear Katherine and Ma and Alfrid, out in the kitchen, talking on and on. Danny was glad that Alfrid could do the explaining to Ma. He wouldn't want to. It was much nicer to lie by the fire and doze.

Katherine's voice interrupted his dream. "Danny, wake up," she said gently. "It's time for us to leave."

Danny fought his way to wakefulness and struggled to his feet. "What about Mundy and the other men in the barn?" he asked.

Katherine put on her coat, rubbing her hands together. "When we get back to St. Joe, we'll send some men to take those three into custody," she said.

Ma strode into the room, dressed to go outside. She was carrying a bundle of clothing. Danny gasped as he recognized his own clothes. "Ma! What are you doing?" he asked.

"I'm moving you back to St. Joseph with me," she said. "Katherine says she'll be glad to have you come and stay."

"But I can't go!" Danny cried. "Alfrid will be all alone!"

"He's a grown man," Ma said. "He can take care of himself. It's you I'm concerned about, love. It's not safe for you here."

"Ma! It was only Dr. Mundy! He'll be put in jail. He won't cause us any more trouble!"

"Trouble? There are troubles all around us. These are dangerous times. If it's not Dr. Mundy causing the trouble, it could be someone else. Danny, I want you with me, where I can keep an eye on you."

Danny flung himself into a chair. "I don't want to go! I want to stay here with my father."

"Danny," Ma began, sudden tears glittering in her eyes.

But Danny suddenly saw a solution to the problem and interrupted, throwing his arms wide. "Ma," he said, "this is a silly thing to argue about—whether I stay here or whether I go with you. There's no more reason for you and Alfrid to wait to get married. Why not do it tomorrow? Then we can all live here together."

For a moment no one spoke. Then Ma answered, her voice sorrowful, "Danny, love, it seems as though I'll be hurting you again. Alfrid and I have decided. We aren't going to marry."

15

DANNY FELT THE horror creep into his chest, and he clenched his hands together. "Ma! I don't believe it!" he stammered. "You—you came out here just to marry Alfrid!"

"Not *just* to marry!" Ma said quickly. "Oh, Danny, love, I missed my children so much, I jumped at the chance to be with you."

As his mother moved toward him, her arms out, Danny backed away from her. "Do you mean you never intended to marry Alfrid?"

"No! That's not what I said. I did intend to marry him, and I had every intention of keeping my promise, but—" Ma grasped for the arm of the nearest chair and plopped into the seat. A tear ran down her nose, and she fumbled in her pocket for a handkerchief. She wiped her eyes and blew her nose, then looked up at Danny with determination. "You may find this hard to understand," she said, "but Alfrid and I—I admire him greatly, but—"

Alfrid had come into the parlor. Now he stepped forward. "Danny," he said, "your mother and I are very different people. While we like each other's company, it is not enough of a foundation on which to build a marriage."

"Melba said that people don't have to love each other to get married!" Danny insisted.

"It makes a marriage stronger if they do," Ma said, and began to blush, red creeping up to stain her cheeks.

Danny stared at her, puzzled. Ma drew Peg to her and held out a hand to Danny, who ignored it. "I have met a man who loves me very much, and I love him," Ma said.

Danny was appalled. "Not that John Murphy!" he shouted.

"Yes," Ma said. "I hope you will wish us happiness. Alfrid has."

"No! I won't!"

Danny fled from the room and dashed upstairs, throwing himself facedown on the bed that was no longer his. He cried in rage and frustration, hitting at the mattress with his fists. Finally, too exhausted to cry any longer, he rolled over on his back and discovered Alfrid patiently sitting in the chair next to the bed.

"Ma's not being fair!" Danny cried out to Alfrid.

"Not fair to whom?" Alfrid asked.

Danny sat up. "Well, to—to you."

"She's been very fair," he said. "She's been honest with me about her feelings for Murphy, and she's paid back every cent of the money I sent for her train fare."

"But she was supposed to marry *you*," Danny moaned.

Alfrid leaned forward, his forearms resting on his knees. "Danny, just between you and me, I am relieved at Noreen's decision. She is a vital, energetic woman, and, truthfully, I want a home that is a place of comfort and peace."

"But Aunt Melba said you should get married."

"One reason was to have someone to care for you and Peg, but now that you won't be living here—" Alfrid's words broke off, and he cleared his throat.

With a cry Danny leapt up and flung his arms around Alfrid. "No matter where I live, you'll still be my father! You will! And I'll think of something. I'll think of a plan. I'll—"

"Danny," Alfrid interrupted, his voice heavy with unhappiness, "it's time for you to go downstairs to join your mother. She and Katherine have been waiting patiently for you. They're ready to leave."

I will think of a plan, Danny promised himself as he walked down the stairs with Alfrid. He couldn't lose another father. He was determined to work out a way.

On the drive back to St. Joseph, Ma put an arm around Danny and hugged him, in spite of the fact that he stiffened, refusing to hug her back. "I couldn't marry a man I don't love just to please my children," she said.

"It doesn't matter," Danny grumbled, spitefully adding, "My father doesn't love *you,* either."

He was sorry he'd said the words the minute they were out of his mouth, but Ma didn't react the way he'd expected. She smiled and said, "See. There you are. It worked out well for the both of us." She hugged him again and added, "Danny, you and John may have—well—got off on the wrong foot with that wild tale you told him about your rowdy brothers and sisters, but I know you'll soon come to like each other."

Danny shook his head. No matter what anyone said, John Murphy had stolen Ma from Alfrid.

They rode the rest of the way in silence.

Danny wasn't to be spared John Murphy's company and conversation. Murphy appeared at Katherine's house the following evening. The moment that he and Danny were alone together, Murphy tilted his head and gave Danny a sardonic grin. "It's a good thing I decided to set things straight with your ma about her wild children," he said. "Honesty turned out to be the best policy."

Danny shrugged and said, "I—I know what I told you wasn't the truth, but I didn't want you to get in the way."

"In the way, is it? Why don't you like me, Danny?"

Danny stared at his shoes. "You're not Alfrid."

"No, I'm not, and thank goodness for that, or your ma would have been bored with me as well."

Danny clenched his fists and glared at Murphy. "Alfrid is *not* boring! He's kind, and he cares about people! And he's not—"

"Hold on now," Murphy said. "Perhaps I was making too light of the situation. A little attempt at humor, you understand."

"What you said wasn't funny."

"Ah, I've got you riled, and I apologize for that," Murphy said. He held out his right hand. "Let's call a truce and start over again. I'd like us to be friends."

Danny grudgingly held out his hand, allowing Murphy to shake it.

"I'm hoping to be friends with your brothers and sisters, too. Sure, I've heard all about them from Noreen and Peg. We're hoping they'll all be able to come to the wedding."

Danny could only stare. Finally he managed to say, "But they'll all be coming here to live, won't they?"

"Well now," Murphy said as he rubbed his chin, "it seems I've blundered again. I should have made sure that Noreen had explained everything to you."

"Explained what?" Danny demanded.

Ma put her hands on Danny's shoulders, and he jumped. He hadn't heard her come up behind him. "It's not that easy, love," she said. "For one thing, the others have been placed into happy homes. They love their foster parents just as you love Alfrid."

"They don't want to come back?" Danny was astounded. As Ma hesitated, something she'd said struck Danny. "You said 'for one thing.' What's the other?"

"Well," Ma began and took a deep breath. "It's hard for a man to take on the care of a wife and *six* children. John has promised me that we'll travel to see the others as often as possible. He said I could go to them anytime they need me, and we'll make a fine home here for you and Peg." She paused as she studied his face. "Danny, we have to be practical. There was no way that Alfrid could have taken us in, either."

"Alfrid didn't say that!"

"We discussed it."

Danny was heartsick. "I don't believe it!"

Murphy's smile vanished. "Don't speak to your ma like that, lad. If she said it's so, then it's so. Alfrid Swenson sent for a wife to care for the two of you children. Isn't that right?"

Numbly, Danny nodded. "We didn't talk about the others coming. I just thought—"

"You've been thinking too much." His tone softened. "Apologize now to your ma, and we'll hear no more about it."

"I'm sorry," Danny whispered.

This wasn't the only apology he had to make, but he hurt so much already that he knew now was the time to take care of the other one. Danny asked Katherine for the loan of paper and pen, and he wrote a letter to Mrs. Pratka explaining all about the so-called shopping list and why he had written it. Then, with a clear conscience but an aching heart, he went to bed.

In the morning Danny asked Katherine to give him a job in her store. "I can only work until school starts again," he said, "and I won't expect to be paid. It's something that—well, it's just something I'd like to do."

Katherine smiled and said, "Most boys would welcome the holiday. You could share the sled I've given to Peg, and there are some young neighbors your age I'd like you to meet."

"I'd rather work in your store," Danny said. He could hardly breathe as he waited for Katherine's answer.

"I suppose you want to stay busy. Well, that's a good way to handle a problem." She smiled and added, "Thank you, Danny. Ask your mother, and if she agrees, you can start work today."

"Of course I agree," Ma said, when Danny told her. "It's a fine way you've thought of to pay Katherine back for her generosity."

Danny knew he was wrong to conceal his reason for wanting to work in the store, but he didn't care. For the first time since Ma told him the awful news, he had something to hope for. Now that he would be working in the store, every time Alfrid came in, he'd be able to see him.

Katherine's general store was a friendly place, filled with the warm fragrance of leather and cinnamon and dried apples and saddle wax. Danny kept busy carrying sacks of salt or flour to the wagons, helping customers find the right nails or boots or bolts of cloth. But all the time he worked he kept glancing at the front door of the store. Each time it opened, he hoped it would be Alfrid who came in.

In the late afternoon of the third day Alfrid did come to the store. Danny ran to greet him, so happy to see Alfrid that his heart was pounding. "It's Wednesday," Danny said. "I knew you'd be in town for the meeting tonight."

"I was planning to come by Katherine's house to see you," Alfrid said. "I've been lonely for you."

"Me too," Danny answered. He fought to keep back the tears that were burning his eyes.

"What have you been doing?" Alfrid asked.

"Doing? Oh, working here at the store. Reading. Not much else." Suddenly he remembered the letter he had written. He fished a rumpled, folded piece of paper from his pocket and handed it to Alfrid. "This is for Mrs. Pratka," Danny said. "Would you give it to her, please?"

Alfrid's eyes twinkled and a corner of his mouth twitched. "Could it be another shopping list?" he asked.

Danny's face grew hot. "You know about the list?"

"Mrs. Pratka heard you had left. She came over to visit, and in the course of our conversation she mentioned it. She knew you had written it and was hurt that you were trying to get rid of her."

"I didn't mean to hurt her feelings," Danny said. "That's why I wrote—to apologize. I tried to explain why I did it. I know it was wrong, and I told her in my letter that I'm sorry." He paused and looked up at Alfrid. "I think she wants to marry you," Danny said.

"I think she does, too," Alfrid agreed. "And maybe that wouldn't be such a bad idea. We're used to each other. She's a pleasant woman, an earnest worker, and a good cook. As Melba said, it's hard for a man to work a farm alone."

Alfrid tucked Danny's letter into his pocket. With a startled look, he pulled out another sheet of paper and unfolded it. "I almost forgot what I came for," he said. He walked to the painted board where people were accustomed to tacking messages.

Danny stepped close to read Alfrid's notice. "You're advertising for a hired hand!" he said.

"Yes," Alfrid told him. "As soon as the heavy snows are over, it will be time to begin to ready the ground for

138

the spring planting." He studied the slip of paper. "Unfortunately, with so many of the young men ready to fight for either the Union or the Confederacy, it may be hard to find one who'd rather put his hand to the plow."

"I know someone!" Danny shouted so loudly that a few of the customers turned to look at him. He ripped down the notice and waved it at Alfrid. "I'll do it!"

Alfrid blinked. "But you're young. You still must go to school."

"I can do the work, too, and school is closed during planting and harvest time."

Alfrid hesitated. "Please," Danny begged. "You said I was as good as any farmhand, and I promise to work hard. I can live on the farm with you and Mrs.—uh—your new wife, and I can see Ma and Peg when I come into town."

"You would really like that, Danny?" Alfrid asked.

"Yes!" Danny said. "I lost one father. Then you became my father. I told you I would never, never lose you, too!"

"And I don't want to lose my son," Alfrid said. "The job is yours." His eyes clouded as he added, "That is, if your mother will give her permission. She was concerned about your safety. She may not agree."

Danny wasn't worried. "Ma was frightened out of her wits Sunday night, but now she'll be thinking more clearly. We'll explain to her that I'm even safer on your farm than I am in the city." He grinned. "I know John Murphy will be more than glad to help talk Ma into agreeing, once he finds that I want to live with you instead of with them."

For the first time Danny saw Alfrid smile. "Which one do you think we should approach first? John Murphy or your mother?"

Danny laughed. "Mr. Murphy," he said quickly. "The three of us will make a plan."

As he left the store with Alfrid, Danny was light-headed with joy. He and Mrs. Pratka would get along well enough—once she'd accepted his apology—and he'd soon come to good terms with Mr. Murphy. He'd have Ma, and he'd have Alfrid, and he'd soon be seeing his brothers and sisters. Danny hadn't known it was possible to be so happy.

16

In LATE MARCH, as the early dogwood was budding, the Kelly children, with their foster families, arrived in St. Joseph for their mother's wedding. The first to fly through Katherine's open front door was Megan, who tried to hug Ma and Danny and Peg all at once.

"Oh, Ma, you're here!" she cried. "And Danny and Peg! I've missed you all so much!"

Danny clung to Megan. "You're blubbering like a baby!" he teased, suddenly aware that his face was wet, too.

"Baby!" Megan pulled back, her tear-streaked face shining. "Oh! Wait till you see our baby!" She jumped to her feet, tugging at her foster mother, beaming at the chubby-cheeked baby in her arms. "Mama, come and meet my Ma. See, Ma! This is Benjamin John. Isn't he wonderful?"

The pain that twisted Ma's face passed so quickly that Danny wondered if he had really seen it. "He's a beautiful child," Ma said, and smiled at Mrs. Browder. "There is no way to thank you enough for all you have done for Megan." Ma smoothed a strand of Megan's hair back from her forehead and let her hand linger as if it were hard to let go.

"No thanks are needed," Mrs. Browder said. "We love Megan." She paused, then added softly, "As you do."

"Thank you," Ma whispered. Then Mr. Browder stepped up to be introduced, and Danny couldn't wait until the newcomers met Alfrid and his wife, Ennie.

In all the hubbub Mike and his foster mother arrived. She was young and pretty and very shy, but she smiled at everyone—especially at Mike, whose shouts and laughter seemed to bounce off the walls of the room. Mike flung himself at Ma, nearly knocking her off her feet.

"How you've grown!" Ma gasped, after she had caught her breath. "You're at least two inches taller!"

"Taller than Danny at last!" Mike said, grinning at his brother.

"Mike!" was all Danny could say. There was so much he wanted to tell Mike, but he choked up and cried against his brother's shoulder, feeling as though he'd never stop.

"Don't take it so hard, lad," Mike teased, but Danny could hear a sob in Mike's laugh, and Mike held tightly to Danny even when Megan and Peg squeezed in for a hug.

"Is your husband with you?" Ma asked Mrs. Taylor. "Mike has written so much about Captain Taylor."

"He wanted to come, but he couldn't," Mrs. Taylor said.

Mike let go of Danny, standing tall, and his face shone with pride. "With the situation between the Union and the Confederacy being so perilous, the Captain's badly needed at the fort," he said.

Mrs. Taylor said to Ma, "We're so proud of Mike. He's a wonderful boy."

"Indeed he is!" Ma said, and Mike looked ready to burst the buttons on his shirt.

Soon Frances and Petey and the Cummingses arrived, and the tears and laughter were so loud and joyful that John Murphy mischievously poked Danny with his elbow and shouted above the uproar. "I do believe you were telling the truth about your noisy brothers and sisters, after all!"

Ma held Frances by the shoulders, searching her face. "You're becoming a beautiful young woman, love," Ma murmured, and tears brimmed from her eyes. "My first child—but you're no longer a child."

Mrs. Cummings stepped forward. "You can be very proud of Frances," she told Ma.

"I've always been proud of Frances Mary," Ma said, and wrapped Frances in her arms. Danny, trying to hug Frances too, heard Ma whisper, "You wrote that now you understand. I didn't know what else to do, love. Do you forgive me? Really forgive me?"

"Oh, Ma," Frances said, burying her face in her mother's shoulder, "there's nothing to forgive! I just love you all the more!"

It wasn't until the next afternoon that the four eldest Kellys were able to be alone together and talk.

Frances Mary came straight out with it. "Danny, do you like Mr. Murphy? Is he a good man? Will he make Ma happy?"

"Yes," Danny said without hesitation. "He's a lot like Da in many ways. He's an outdoors kind of man. He's strong, he's got a good disposition, he likes to laugh, and he can make Ma laugh."

"Are you telling us the all of it?" Frances looked at him closely. "If everything about Mr. Murphy is to the good, then why don't you want to live with him?"

"Because he isn't Alfrid," Danny said.

143

Mike nodded. "I know what he means. I can't imagine living anywhere but with Captain Taylor and his wife. I've met no better man than Captain Taylor. As a matter of fact, I'm thinking of an army career myself."

Danny hooted and poked Mike in the ribs. "Army career! You're not old enough."

Mike didn't laugh and push him back, as Danny had expected. Instead, Mike answered seriously, "The army will be needing drummer boys to go into battle with the troops."

"Mike!" Megan gasped and clutched his arm. "You wouldn't! You could get killed! Surely the captain wouldn't let you!"

Mike shrugged. "You're right. He doesn't think much of the idea." Quickly, he changed the subject, asking, "Megan, do you like living out on the prairie so far from everyone?"

Megan smiled and began to tell them all how much she loved the prairie and her foster family, but Danny's mind was still on Mike. He'd seen that guarded look in his eyes.

"It's hard to believe. We each have two families to belong to now," Frances said.

"Would you want to live with Ma again?" Megan asked her.

Frances thought a long minute, the others studying her face, before she spoke. "I love Ma with all my heart," she said. "Not long ago I didn't know how I could get through each day without her. But now—well, it's as though I can see more clearly. I can love Ma just as much as I ever did, but I can love my foster parents, too. Do you understand?"

Megan nodded. "The more people you love, the more love you have to give."

"It's not like having to make a choice," Mike added. "It's like having all of the best."

144

"It's strange to think of Ma getting married, though," Frances said. "I had to get used to the idea. I wasn't sure I liked it."

"Ma's no different from us," Danny told her. "Megan said it. Now Ma's got more people to love, too."

"Murphy seems like a good egg," Mike said.

Danny nodded. "Don't worry. I'll keep an eye on him."

Frances and Megan laughed, and Mike said, "That's enough talk about Ma's wedding. I've got some good stories I heard at the fort. There's a one-eyed soldier there who told me how he knocked two charging renegade Indians off their horses with only one shot." Mike leaned forward and lowered his voice. "It was in the dark of night, with only the campfires for lights ..."

The next morning—a morning as clear and sunny as though it had been ordered—Noreen Kelly, wearing a new dress of the palest blue, married John Murphy. All her children and their foster families were in attendance. Mike, who had accepted Murphy immediately with the words "It's a good thing the man is Irish," escorted his mother up the aisle of the small church to stand before the priest.

Danny, dressed in new trousers and coat, stood proudly by John Murphy's side. "Although you've got a long way to go to become a man," Murphy had told Danny with a grin and a wink, "you're old enough to sign your name to a document, and I can't think of anyone I'd rather have as a witness." Danny was pleased to see that of the lot, Murphy was the most nervous.

Frances, Megan, and Peg stood next to Ma, each of them holding a small bouquet of early crocus and snowdrops from Katherine's garden. Frances and Megan had tears in their eyes, but Peg was ecstatic with excitement and kept jumping up and down trying to see everything.

With a sideways glance, Danny checked on Petey, who seemed content. He was snuggled up against Mrs. Cummings, who kept looking down to beam at him.

The prayers seemed to last a very long time. Finally Murphy said, "With this ring I thee wed," and Danny snapped to attention. He was supposed to be a witness to this wedding, and he'd been letting his mind wander.

"Whom God has joined together, let no man put asunder," Danny heard the priest say.

The people in the church began murmuring and smiling at each other and at Ma, whose face shone so brightly with happiness that Danny had a fleeting moment of guilt for ever wanting to keep her and Mr. Murphy apart.

Katherine stepped up to hug Ma. Andrew was right behind her. They looked as radiantly happy as the just-married couple.

The Kellys gathered around to kiss their mother and shake hands with Mr. Murphy, wishing them well. Then, as one, they drifted to the side of the church, away from the happy group with Ma in the center.

"What about us?" Frances said. She reached out and grasped Megan's hand. "The states will be involved in war soon. There's no doubt about it. I wonder if—*when*—we'll see each other again. I wonder what our destiny will be."

Megan put an arm around her sister's shoulders. "I can promise you we'll be together again," she said firmly. "Our destiny is going to be whatever we make it."

"And no matter where it takes us," Mike said, that faraway look in his eyes again.

"I agree with Megan," Danny said. "Things always work out the way they should." He paused and added, "That is, if you have a plan."

As Grandma closed the journal, Jennifer gave a disappointed sigh. "So that's the all of it," she said.

"Oh, no," Grandma answered smiling. "The stories I've told you are really just the beginning. War was declared, and of course it affected all of their lives."

Jeff asked, "Did Mike join the army as a drummer boy and go into battle, Grandma?"

Jennifer turned to him and answered first. "Don't you remember Jeff? Mike told his sisters that Captain Taylor didn't want him to."

"I think we've had enough today," said Grandma. "I'm not going to tell you what Mike did just yet."

Jennifer and Jeff stared at her. "I bet Mike ran away to join the army," Jeff said. "Did he? Why won't you tell us? Please."

Grandma smiled. "It's a long story. What Mike did and what the other Kellys did belong in other stories for other days."

"Are those stories in the journal?" Jennifer asked.

"Oh, my, yes," Grandma explained, "You certainly wouldn't want me to spoil things by telling you in advance what happened to Mike or to his friend Jim, who got mixed up with a riverboat gambler on his way to find Mike. Or to Peg, who was trapped inside a cave with an outlaw; or to Frances and her friend Carrie when they found themselves in the path of General Sterling Price and his Raiders."

Jeff groaned, "Grandma, don't do that to us!"

Grandma laughed. "You're right. I shouldn't tease you. To make amends I suppose I'd better tell you another story."

"Great!" Jennifer said. "When?"

The twinkle in Grandma's eyes was unmistakably mischievous. "Not now, of course," she said and put the journal safely away. "Tomorrow."

About the Author

JOAN LOWERY NIXON is the acclaimed author of more than sixty fiction and non-fiction books for children and young adults. She is a three-time winner of the Mystery Writers of America Edgar Award and the recipient of many Children's Choice awards. Her popular books for young adults include the first three books in the Orphan Train Quartet, *A Family Apart, Caught in the Act,* and *In the Face of Danger,* as well as *The Kidnapping of Christina Lattimore, The Specter,* and *The Seance.* She was moved by the true experiences of the children on the nineteenth-century orphan trains to research and write the Orphan Train Quartet.

Mrs. Nixon and her husband live in Houston, Texas.

Copy 1

NIX   Copy 1

Nixon, Joan Lowery
The Orphan Quartet
A Place to Belong #4

	DATE DUE	
OCT 17 '91	JAN 19 '93	
OCT 24 '91	FEB 01 '93	
OCT 31 '91	MAR 15 '93	
NOV 7 '91	De Mattos	
NOV 21 '91	SEP 30 1993 OCT 07 '93	
JAN 2 1992		
JAN 9 1992		
JAN 23 1992		
FEB 6 1992		
MAR 19 1992		
Pond (vol)